GHOST OF
A CHANCE

THE BEELER LARGE PRINT MYSTERY SERIES

Edited by Audrey A. Lesko

GHOST OF
A CHANCE

Helen Chappell

BEELER LARGE PRINT
Hampton Falls, New Hampshire, 1999

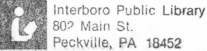

Library of Congress Cataloging-in-Publication Data

Chappell, Helen 1947–
  Ghost of a chance / Helen Chappell.
     p.   cm. — (The Beeler large print mystery series)
  ISBN 1-57490-202-4 (hardcover : alk. paper)
  1. Large type books. I. Title. II. Series.
  [PS3553.H299G47 1999]
  813'.54—dc21   98-50925
                                          CIP

Published in Large Print by arrangement with
Dell Publishing, a division of Random House, Inc.

BEELER LARGE PRINT
is published by
Thomas T. Beeler, *Publisher*
Post Office Box 659
Hampton Falls, New Hampshire 03844

Typeset in 16 point Times New Roman type.
Printed on acid-free paper and bound by
BookCrafters in Chelsea, Michigan.

ACKNOWLEDGMENTS

Thanks are once again due to the usual suspects: To Peter Whitesell, M.D., who literally saved my life, to Kathryn Pearce and Nancy Yost and to my editor Jacquie Miller, who actually thinks I'm funny, many thanks. Chief Wade Roche once again came through like the former state trooper he is, with inspiration, corrections, suggestions, great stories, forensic pathology, and really grisly photos. Anyone who thinks I make this stuff up ought to talk to Wade. Thanks to the Hon. William S. Horne, for thinking *Dead Duck* is funny. Again, Arlene Chase and Karen Basile read, edited, commented, and held my hand. And thanks to all my students, who read my books and have a chance to ring me back. Last, a very special thanks to Anne Stinson, who found the Ornamental Hermit. If you like this book, the credit goes to all of the folks named herein. All mistakes are mine. Thank you one and all. You're great.

GHOST OF
A CHANCE

CHAPTER 1

IT SEEMED LIKE A GOOD IDEA AT THE TIME

BEING A GHOST, I HAVE DISCOVERED, GIVES YOU certain advantages.

Of course, being dead is no chicken cruise, as you, dear reader, will inevitably discover. But all in all, I, Sam Wescott have found being a haunt much more interesting than being alive.

I wish I could say that my former wife, Hollis Ball, agrees with me about my changed position in the world But she tends to view my living-impaired status with suspicion, sometimes even with hostility, as if I died deliberately.

Well, actually, now that I think about it, I did, but that's another story.

I suppose her lack of understanding is a female thing. Women are something no man, alive or dead, has ever been able to figure out.

Since my death I have been assigned by The Powers That Be to haunt her. Well, haunt . . . that's kind of a tough word. Say the word haunt, people think of rattling chains and tortured shrieks and things going bump in the night. Not my way of doing business at all.

My job, in payment for the way I panicked at commitment and abandoned Hollis in life, is to work off my sins as a sort of guardian angel. When she'll let me.

You see, Hollis is of the do-it-yourself school, and as stubborn and hardheaded an Eastern Shorewoman as you could find. But she's from Beddoe's Island, the Stubborn, Hardheaded Woman Capital of Chesapeake

1

Bay. She's a reporter for a local newspaper, the *Watertown Gazette*, and has had little time for ghosts or any other fun stuff, at least until I reappeared in her life.

Haunting Hollis is difficult, to say the least. For one thing, she never listens to me, and she should, oh, she really should.

Folks, I am paying with usurious interest for my previous bad behavior. Face it Looking after this woman is a job of work.

Left to her own devices Hollis might have missed the story entirely. After all, she's only human, and if you ask me, more human than some. If it weren't for me she would have missed the whole adventure we had with the Ornamental Hermit. . .

It was a terrific April morning, one of those days that comes as a blessing after the Eastern Shore winter, to which the climate of hell's north gate has been favorably compared.

Warmth turned the yellow-green buds the colors of fire, and there was just enough air to fill a sail. So did Hollis call in sick and run off to take advantage of this glorious day?

You'd better believe she did.

When I located her she was on hegira, headed toward the beach, propelling her ancient Honda Civic north toward Rehobeth, over in Delaware. When she should have been in court covering the dullest civil trial in the history of civil law, tsk, tsk! The Beach Boys blared from the tape deck; and it was clear that Holl was hell-bent on having fun fun fun till Daddy took the T-Bird away.

When I was alive there was nothing I loved more than cars—unless it was boats and women. But, of course, a

2

really cool car is a babe magnet. I still can feel the ancient male excitement when I see a really fine Porsche or a classic MG. Just because you're dead doesn't mean your testosterone dries up.

Hollis, on the other hand, persists in driving this ancient piece of Japanese tin that has been on its last legs since the odometer turned 200,000 miles many, many road trips ago. Not just that, but it's a traveling wastebasket. The back is almost completely filled up with old newspapers, burger wrappers, discarded notebooks, promotional gimmes, and God only knows what other trash from a small-town reporter's life. I mean to say it is pretty gross. It smells like an old cigarette, even though she has valiantly been struggling with not smoking since she was trapped in that decoy fire and got her lungs filled up with more poison on top of all that nicotine.

Even as I was musing on our last outing, I saw her reach for a cigarette butt in the ashtray and decided it was time to make myself known.

"You promised," I tsked as I solidified myself in the passenger seat. "You're on the patch!"

Hollis jerked as if she had been struck with a rolled-up newspaper. She snatched her hand away from the ashtray and glared at me as we nearly ran off the two-lane blacktop into a soybean field.

"Dammit, Sam, don't startle me like that!" she yelled, righting the car. "I hate it when you just show up like that!" She pressed a hand on her heart. "Especially when I'm taking a day off from everything. Including you! Mostly you! What are you doing here?"

"A simple hello would be nice, you know," I replied, having floated down to seat level. You'd think she'd be glad to see me, wouldn't you? After all, when I show up

3

in her life things always become much more interesting. Instead of reminding her of this fact, I got right to business. Time, after all, was of the essence.

"There's something happening up ahead at Calais Road Bridge, on the state line. A car in the water. They sent for the ambulance, and the cops from both Maryland and Delaware are there now. Sounds like a story to me, but, of course, I'm not a reporter. You may want to spend the rest of your day listening to these old farts drone on, but if I were you—"

"Are you sure, or is this one of your stupid ghost tricks?" Hollis demanded as she gathered up all the Altoids mints that had spilled out of her pocketbook. I really can't understand why she never trusts me. After all, my postmortal hearing is remarkably acute. I can hear a police scanner in the next county if I want to.

"I'm sure," I replied, doing my best to look utterly honest. "Sounds like a story to me."

Hollis frowned, thinking it over. Why won't she take my word for anything? Just because I had a small history of being ever so slightly unreliable when we were married?

I floated up, then stretched out over the trashed backseat, yawning. "I'll bet the Call *has already heard the scanner and their reporter's on the way."* Mentioning the Gazette's rival paper usually prods her into action. *"Of course, you could cut across through Federalsburg to Georgetown and avoid the whole thing entirely. I'm sure the beach is great today. Of course, it's still a little windy and chilly, but . . ."*

She bit her lip, and a very pretty lip it is too. The idea of losing a story is anathema to her. "Well, if you're sure," she muttered grudgingly, stuffing mints and reportorial odds and ends back into her pocketbook

4

with one hand while the other was on the wheel. I wish she wouldn't do that.

I was about to say that her attempt to stop smoking, however commendable, was making her quite irritable, then I thought better of it. No needs to fight with a recovering nicotine addict? It's so unsporting.

"Calais Bridge?" she asked me again. "Are you sure?"

"Sure as I float here," I reassured her from the back. "Can I drive?"

"No!" She turned the wheel and we headed into our next big adventure. "My insurance does not cover ghosts!"

Silly woman.

CHAPTER 2

THE SACRED CADILLAC BURIAL GROUND

AS WE APPROACHED THE CALAIS BRIDGE, A NARROW concrete span built in the days of the W.P.A., I counted four trucks and three ambulances from five different fire companies, an Advanced Life Support van, four Department of Natural Resources 4x4s, seven unmarked pickups, and about seven or eight police cruisers from Maryland and Delaware. A big wrecker was backed up to the edge of the boat launch, its heaviest come-along chain stretched from the winch out into the water, where it disappeared into the black current.

There were more people in uniform milling around the old bridge than you might reasonably expect to see at a modest war, and most of them were doing little more than hanging over the low sides, staring

5

expectantly into the swirling green Santimoke River, watching as it rolled downstream toward Chesapeake Bay.

Up here the river was narrow, no more than a hundred feet wide from bank to bank. But it was also deep—hence the treacherous currents, made even more dangerous by the tidal flows that ebbed and flowed around the marshes.

I could see them, of course, but none of them could see me. They grudgingly gave way as Hollis reached the middle of the bridge, where an all-too-familiar face watched her progress from behind a glum expression.

"Hey, Hollis, you're just in time!" growled Detective Sergeant Ormand Friendly of the Maryland State Police. "All we needed was a reporter on the scene to make things complete," he added sourly to the man standing beside him.

"Oh, bite me, Ormand," Hollis murmured cheerfully. Aloud, she said without missing a beat, "Lieutenant Cropper, how nice to see you again! What's going on, Friendly? Accident?"

"Ask Lieutenant Cropper," Friendly said, indicating the tall, thin man standing beside him, who wore a plastic ID that proclaimed him a member of the First State's motor-vehicle crimes squad. "Looks like Delaware's tossed us the ball on this one," he sighed.

As usual, Friendly sounded as if he were about to blow up. A native Baltimoron, he has little or no understanding of how things work on this side of the Bay, but in spite of their professional hostility, Hollis is actually dating this quasi-human lunk. She says he looks like Harrison Ford, if Harrison Ford had been ridden hard and put away wet, but I personally can't see it. Given my mild youthful indiscretions that unfortunately

6

sometimes involved law enforcement, you can't really blame me for an intrinsic dislike of cops. But then again, unkind souls have suggested that I have always had a problem with authority. While Hollis has been seeing Friendly socially, they are not sleeping together—yet. Nor will they if I can help it The man irks me, and I have a feeling, if he knew of my existence, the feeling would be mutual.

"Well, it would appear that the accident happened on the Maryland side of the state line." Lieutenant Cropper was saying apologetically. He had the look of a man who has only a few years to a decent retirement pension and doesn't want to do anything to jeopardize it. "Delaware doesn't begin until you walk up the road about five hundred yards," he pointed out, indicating the state-line sign on the other side of Calais Bridge. "We are cooperating with manpower and equipment, Sergeant," he added, a trifle heavily.

Friendly had the grace to duck his head. "Sorry," he mumbled. "But you can understand that this is just about the last thing we needed, what with that crack bust last week . . ."

Old news. "So!" Hollis said quickly, whipping out her notebook; all business again. "What's the story here, gentlemen?"

"Well, they're about to replace this old bridge with a new one. The construction company's divers were down there this morning, looking at the pilings and the pier, when they spotted a car down below," Lieutenant Cropper explained.

"Big old tail-fin job, buried in the mud at the bottom of the channel," Friendly said in tones approaching wonder. "No telling how it got there, or how long it's been there neither, but they think it's been years."

7

"Probably stolen, then run off the bridge," Cropper remarked. He looked around. "Probably been down there a good while, too, from what the divers said, She's worked her way pretty deep into the mud. If it weren't for the tail fins stickin' up, no one woulda seen it."

"Don't see any skid marks, and the bridge rails aren't damaged," Friendly said. "So it didn't go overboard today."

A real Sherlock Holmes, this one. What does Hollis see in him, aside from the obvious testosterone?

"Like the Detective Sergeant says, the divers think it's been down there a while," Cropper observed, carefully backing up a fellow officer. "One o' them big ol' tail-fin jobs too, from the sixties! The divers say she was almost completely buried down in that mud bottom, so she's had to have been there for a while, but we don't know anything more than that till we get her winched up out of there and on dry land." He gestured toward the wrecker. "We've got some Natural Resources divers down there now, chainin' 'er up so she can be hauled out. It's a job of work too. Thing must weigh about five or six tons with all the mud and water."

As an invisible entity I could go places where a mortal would be turned away, so I decided to cruise the scene to find out what I could. If I had known that Detective Sergeant Ormand Friendly was going to be here, I brooded, I never would have talked Hollis into stopping, not even if Martians had landed here.

Being a ghost doesn't give you unlimited psychic powers, however. I'd be willing to bet that Batman can do cooler stuff than I can, and he's a fictional character. Besides, I'm still learning this ghost stuff. You'd think when The Powers That Be make you a ghost they'd give you an instruction booklet, but it's mostly trial and error Or, as Ed Poe says, trial and terror.

Calais Road is a two-lane blacktop that starts in Watertown and winds upcounty from the Bay, through soybean fields and farmland, north toward the state line. If you stay on it long enough you end up in Delaware Bay. Long ago, back before the Revolutionary War, there was a Huguenot settlement here named Calais, after the French port, but it dried up and blew away two hundred years ago. All that's left is a bridge and a long, lonely stretch of marsh, framed by the spread of distant farms over the hills.

It looked to me as if every morbid curiosity seeker in the tricounty area had congregated here, with all their attention focused on something happening in the water. They crammed themselves as close to the crown of the bridge as the cops would allow, staring intently down at the current, pointing and exclaiming, as humans are wont to do at the scene of a tragedy. I shuddered at the glazed, greedy look in their eyes, that bloodthirsty sort of look people get at accidents, crime scenes, and public executions. Makes me glad to be dead and past all—or at least most—of that stuff.

While Hollis was prodding Friendly and Lieutenant Cropper for information, I slid easily through solid trucks and yellow crime-scene tape to the top of the bridge and looked down at the swirling waters. I saw nothing but swift current and a deep, treacherous channel, what were these people waiting for?

"They got it! Throw 'er on, Bruce! Throw 'er on!" The wrecker's winch suddenly screamed to life on the starboard side of the Jersey wall, and two more guys began feeding the heavy chain down to the water's edge, where it disappeared into the dark waters.

Suddenly, the chain began to tighten, pulling taut out

of the water.

The onlookers cheered and whistled.

"Renata Ringwood Clinton," someone said. It was no more than a whisper, or perhaps just a thought. Sometimes I get the two confused. Over here, on this side of reality, the five senses are often confusing and intense. I looked around. I saw her for only a moment, the faintest incandescent outline of her, but I knew at once she was a ghost; we know our own by the signs. A woman with a hard expression and a stiffened mass of dark hair, her big hoop earrings glittered in the sunlight. She stood a few feet away from me, watching the car emerge into the air. Then she sensed my stare and met my look through eyes rimmed with thick black liner. "They finally found it," she said, amused. She glanced at the car. "It's been down there in the water for so long, so very long," she said matter-of-factly. "It was so cold down there."

There was a shout, and the crowd began to applaud and cheer. Just then the wrecker's winch started to whine, and the chain pulled up taut from the water, bearing the terrible weight of some great and unseen bulk.

As we watched, the tail fins of a midcentury monster mobile slowly broke water and began an inexorable, majestic crawl toward dry land The winch on the wrecker screamed louder, straining against the enormous weight.

I sensed Hollis arguing with Friendly for information and permission to move in closer to the site. "Come on, Ormand!" she was pleading. "It's not like this is a fresh scene or anything!"

Suddenly, a slick black head broke the surface of the river, and a diver pushed back his goggles to reveal his human face. He treaded water for a moment, looking around, then was joined by a second diver Both swam free of the path of the car as it rose from the river, dripping with slime and the encrusted patina of oxide. It slowly progressed toward dry land, and when the tail-finned behemoth was finally dragged up on the landing, there was a collective sigh from the observers. It was as if some long-buried and forgotten treasure from an ancient civilization had been rediscovered.

"You got her now!" the crowd was calling. Some people were even cheering. "Go! Go! Go!"

With a watery crunch the car settled. Water and corrosion poured out of her, running down the asphalt toward the river, and she sank, like a tired fat woman, into dry land.

"Holy shit!" A young man in volunteer fire department waders standing near me cursed in stunned awe beneath his breath. He probably had not even been thought of, let alone born, when this baby rolled off an assembly line in Detroit, smelling of newness and the American dream. But even he could respect this magnificent dinosaur of an automobile, the 1958 Coupe de Ville. "Well, holy shit," he repeated reverently.

You could see that it had once been bright red, but now it was the color of dried blood beneath a crust of river mud and barnacles. The hood was open and the exposed engine looked like the entrails of an ancient monster, but it was still a magnificent car.

"Hey, Loot!" the first diver called, gesturing wildly toward Friendly and Cropper. "We got a whole lot more'n a hot car here!"

"There's some bones inside that Caddy!" the second diver shouted, pulling off his mask so that the whites of his frightened eyes were visible. He drew in a deep

11

breath, treading water. "Human bones!"

As her translucent form blended into the vernal air, the black-haired ghost sighed and faded away. Then I knew it was her body they'd found in the Cadillac.

CHAPTER 3

DEAD MAN SQUAWKING

EVEN A JONAH CAN HAVE A PIECE OF LUCK. THE Cadillac story made the front page above the fold the next day. It looked good and read well, mostly because Rig Riggle, the editor from hell, hadn't touched it.

I had just finished my morning rounds and written my daily crime and accident report seconds before the ancient and overloaded computer system in the *Gazette* newsroom crashed yet again.

While Rig lurched about in a tizzy—his usual behavior in a crisis—I muttered something about court, snuck out, and made for my car. It was a gorgeous day, and the beach still beckoned.

After you've seen a vintage Caddy pulled out of the Santimoke River, anything else that is likely to happen that week will be an anticlimax.

With a long, leisurely lunch at the Back Porch, an afternoon of browsing the sales at the Baltimore Avenue boutiques, and a long walk on the beach calling to me, I was in a mood to tell everyone I would be in court all afternoon and disappear.

I almost made it past the reception desk and out the front door when Jolene—the office snitch/Rig's mistress/social-page editor—caught me. Believe me, you don't want a hyphenated job description at the

12

Gazette.

"Telephone, Hol-lis," she sang, holding out the receiver with one fake-nailed hand while applying a thick frame of lip liner with the other.

Reluctantly, I stopped and took the phone, aware that she would be listening to every word.

"Miss Ball?" asked an oddly familiar voice that I couldn't place.

"Speaking."

"This is Billy Chinaberry. I just read my morning paper and I saw your story about the Cadillac comin' up out of the river."

"Who is this really?" I demanded impatiently.

There was a crackle at the other end of the wire. "Oh, this's Billy Chinaberry all right," he said, vastly amused.

Well, it sure sounded like him. That nasal voice was hard to mistake. Yes, *that* Billy Chinaberry. The Poultry Prince of TV-commercial fame. He's the one who dresses up like Henry VIII, complete with doublet and crown, to push his birds to the Great American Public. Surely, you have seen his "Chicken Fit for a King" shtick or eaten a Royal Poultry Packer, a roasting chicken the size of a Volkswagen? Yes, that Prince of Poultry. Chinaberry's Royal chickens, many of them raised right here on Maryland's lovely Eastern Shore, were the country's number-one-selling feather meat. Until his recent retirement and Royal Farms' merger with Mammon Foods International, Chinaberry's relentless promotion of his product had made him a household celebrity. *Be the queen of your kitchen, says the Prince of Poultry! Serve the family a Royal Farms Poultry Packer!*

Obviously, this was an impostor. For one thing,

13

celebrity chicken magnates just don't call me. I peered at Jolene, who was sitting there with her magenta lips hanging open in awe. "This is a joke, isn't it? Who put you up to this?" I couldn't see around the corner, but I fully expected the boys from the printing plant to pop out of nowhere, shouting "Surprise!" and "Gotcha!"

"I assure you, this is no joke. This is, however, something of an emergency. I am Billy Chinaberry, and you are, I take it, Hollis Ball?" the Prince of Pullets demanded importantly. That voice, like the *bawking* of a chicken, was impossible to imitate.

I squinted at the phone. "It really *is* you," I said, gaping like the stupidest of the very stupid talk-show guests. The boys wouldn't be able to pull off that imperious air. Only the very rich and the very powerful can do that.

"I'll come right to the point, Ms. Ball," he said briskly. "I am a great admirer of your writing in the *Gazette*."

I blushed. Prettily, I hoped. "Uh, th-thanks," I stammered. "But what . . ."

Chinaberry sucked in his breath. "Always look for your byline," he growled. "I read three dailies and *The Wall Street Journal* every day, and you're good. Good writing is hard to come by. I'm willing to pay for what I want."

"And that is?"

"Come on out to Water Garden and we'll discuss that. When are you free?"

I had a mental picture of Rehobeth flying away across the ocean on chicken wings. "I could be free right now," I replied.

"Good. I'll expect you in twenty minutes." He gave me directions and hung up the phone in my ear.

14

A real class act, I thought.

But I went anyway.

I once wrote a story on the shore's highway that opened, "Route 50 cuts through the fields and marshlands of the Eastern Shore like a raw and bleeding artery." Rig had cut it out lest it offend the real-estate advertisers.

Route 50 East was bumper to bumper: a clog of drunken teenagers on their way to spring break in Ocean City, packs of eighteen-wheelers trying to get to the Bay Bridge-Tunnel without being weighed, lumbering tour buses looking for the quaint and charming, stewing locals just trying to get from one town to the next without becoming a highway statistic.

"Just follow the chicken houses," Sam chattered, nodding at the two-story pole buildings that dotted the landscape of Devanau County. "What's the deal with those anyway? You own the land, the poultry producer comes in and builds the chicken house, gives you the baby chickens. You buy the feed and raise them, and you get a percentage of the profit per bird?"

"Something like that." I frowned. "I'm not real sure. All I know is, I wouldn't want to be a chicken in one of those places."

"It's not a happy-camper industry—if you're the main course." Sam hummed through his teeth, drumming noiselessly on his thighs.

"Why are you so nervous?" I asked, slamming on the brakes as a Grand Cherokee full of partying teens from Glen Burnie suddenly cut in inches away from my bumper. If they were fifteen minutes late arriving at Big Pecker's, the beach might disappear.

"Future ghosts," Sam said nonchalantly. "You wouldn't believe how many highway ghosts there

15

are. . . ."

"Sam, what's bothering you? You're not yourself. Well, you're never yourself, but you are really not yourself right now."

"Ah, I'm okay," he muttered, in that tone all men, living or dead, use when they're really *not* okay.

"Come on, Sam. What's bothering you?" I asked. "Is it something about Billy Chinaberry? Did you know him or something? Did you do something to him too?"

Sam shook his head, and the drumming picked up a faster rhythm. "It's nothing. I gotta go."

He faded quickly into nothingness.

It suddenly occurred to me that if you want to get rid of a man, alive or dead, the thing to do is ask him to discuss his feelings with you. Would that I had figured this out earlier in my career.

I glanced behind me in the rearview mirror. The same black car had been on my bumper since I'd left Watertown. Obviously, a beachgoer in a hurry. Then why didn't he pass me?

I saw the road I wanted and signaled a turn. As I thankfully slid off the highway to hell, the black car followed. When the car pulled into a village gas station, I felt easier. My imagination was getting to me.

After navigating a series of narrow back roads and passing lots of farms with those big, big chicken houses, I finally stumbled across Chez Chinaberry almost by accident.

I think it was the brick pillars on either side of the drive that gave it away. Each was surmounted with a giant marble Rhode Island Red. A rooster and a hen, no less.

The long driveway was shaded by a groomed tunnel of ancient tulip poplars. On either side of the lane, solid

16

banks of daffodils and hyacinths, planted in geometric rows, stretched away, ending in deep shrub borders beneath the trees. In the first bloom of spring the flowers' yellow, white, and purple heads nodded gently on the breeze. Part of me wanted to get out and pick an armload to carry home with me; a bouquet of these would brighten my house considerably.

But greater wonders were in store.

I finally pulled up in front of a large, rambling white house, surrounded by carefully tended rose beds and ancient magnolias that sheltered well-manicured lawns. Brick pathways wound around and disappeared into arbors and artfully constructed low walls, over which weeping cherries and flowering peach trees bent their long, fingery branches. Here and there, imposing marble statuary rose from the shrubbery. Diana at the hunt and small putti raised sightless white eyes toward the sunny sky. An angel reached toward heaven, and a saint surveyed the bed of red tulips at her feet.

It was like being in an English park or one of those garden catalogs. I'd never seen anything like this in a private home before, and it made me question my notions of Billy Chinaberry, the Poultry Prince.

Whoever tended to the landscaping here did a job of work, I thought as I parked beside a Lincoln Town Car. Everything looked immaculate, right down to the well-mulched border of crocuses blooming around the front walk, fronted by two Japanese dogwoods just coming into bloom.

I walked up a shallow set of brick steps and rang the bell. I was not especially surprised to see a well-polished brass chicken on the door knocker,

A housekeeper in a white uniform let me in. She seemed totally incurious at my sudden appearance.

"He's expecting you," she said when I told her my name. "He's back in the greenhouses."

As I followed her down the hallway I peered into rooms that seemed to be more comfortable than elegant. Vases full of orchid blossoms caught the eye everywhere, and their musky scent filled the air.

"Mr. Chinaberry just loves his flowers," the woman chuckled when she saw me pause before a delft pagoda stuffed with several varieties of yellow and red tulips. "Keeps me busy arrangin' 'em all. He even sent me to florist school over in Washington to learn how to do all the fancy arrangements."

"Does he live here all alone?" I ventured to ask, since we never passed another human being in all those winding corridors.

"He does now," the housekeeper confided. "Since the last Mrs. Chinaberry left last year. He said, 'No more wives,' and that was that. No children either, poor man. No one should be all alone like that at the end."

"The end?" I repeated, uncertain that I had heard her correctly.

She clucked, as if she had said too much, and picked up her pace. "Mr. Chinaberry's in there somewheres," she said, opening a glass door off what appeared to be a study. I only had time to see a fancy Macintosh with all the bells and whistles before she nodded me on.

I looked into a greenhouse filled with the heavy smell of green and growing things. The heat and humidity were like a slap after the coolness of the house. I turned, but the housekeeper had shut the door firmly behind herself and disappeared. I peered into a jungle of staghorn ferns, banana trees, and palm foliage before taking a step farther. It felt as if the tangle of vegetation had swallowed me up; I had entered a miniature rain

18

forest.

From somewhere I heard the strains of a Chopin piano étude. Water dripped from the fronds of an aralia, splattering my head. "Mr. Chinaberry?" I called uncertainly.

"Over here," called a muffled voice, and I followed a narrow dirt path through the ficuses. Spider-plant drops brushed at my face from above, and the thick, rotten smell of moistness and moss filled my nose.

I emerged to discover a vast spread of growing benches, filled with row after orderly row of small terra-cotta pots. There must have been a hundred of them, arranged like soldiers in formation. Out of each one a single stem with a single bud emerged. They were all tulips, I noticed.

"Thank you for coming." Chinaberry, in butcher's apron and gloves, was standing at a gardener's bench, examining a pot containing a single tulip bloom. He smiled wearily, and I noted the waxy pallor of his skin and the deep purple blotches under his eyes. As he pulled off a gardening glove to shake my hand, I saw the tremors in his fingers and got a good look at him in the light.

Tall and thin, late sixties, early seventies, balding, with a beak of a nose and deep-set, beady eyes. He really did look like a rooster. A rooster with a lot of money and a waxy sheen to his skin.

"Come take a look at this," he said, gesturing me to come closer to the bulb he was examining at the workbench. "I think this may come very close to being the best black tulip I've ever bred. Of course, I'm only an amateur at this, but note the darkness of the calyx. Hopefully, when it opens it will be an ink black rather than a deep purple. I do wonder about the perianth

19

though; will it be bilaterally symmetrical, do you think? There is every chance it will be irregular," he fretted.

To me it just looked like an ugly bud, but what do I know?

"Tulips are a particular hobby of mine," he explained. "Although I love gardening in general, it's the bulbs and corms that truly hold my interest. These are my tulips," he gestured around the tables. "I'm especially proud of my species bulbs this year. I think adding a little nitrogen to the mix last fall really made a difference. I've gotten some wonderful results with the Johann Strausses and the Flaming Parrots." He gestured toward some yellow and red buds.

"Very pretty," I agreed.

"Although you may prefer the Clusiana, or even the Maytime. Many people like the pinks best. Emperors may be shorter in stem, but they're a fine addition in any low border, I think. And early too. These Emperors will go out first." As he spoke he waved his trowel across the rows of potted blooms. "Did you know that the Dutch so valued their tulips that they used to speculate on them, the way we trade on soybeans or pork bellies? Huge fortunes were made and lost on tulip bulbs in the Netherlands in the seventeenth century, when the bulbs first came there from Turkey. They're native to Turkey, did you know that?"

I didn't.

"A rare hybrid can still bring in an enormous amount of money from a breeder. The bulb companies spend enormous amounts of money developing new strains and employ high security to make certain that no industrial thief steals their research or their bulbs. They even patent their hybrids so no one else can propagate them."

He winked at me, and I wondered if he had ever trafficked in stolen bulbs. Collectors, I've found to my cost, will do anything.

"That was one of the things that distressed me the most in the army, back during the war. The Dutch resources had been so depleted by the Nazi occupation that they were reduced to eating tulip bulbs." He shook his head. "Do you know how many experimental hybrids were lost that way?"

I shook my head.

"Hundreds, no doubt." Chinaberry sighed, peering closely at his single black tulip. "While it is not as horrific as many of the atrocities the Nazis committed, of course, it is another loss to the world. Piet Van der Mies, for instance, ate all thirty varieties of experimental dark-petaled hybrids he had been working on when the Germans overran Holland. Although he held out for months, in the end the basic human desire to survive overcame his great passion for botany. He sliced them, boiled them with a sliver of black-market pork fat, and managed to survive."

I followed Chinaberry down the aisle between the rows of tulips. "Coming on, of course, I'll have lilies and begonias, but they won't be ready to transplant until the middle of May . . . ." He stopped, and I stopped behind him. "Van der Mies created seventeen of the most beautiful dark tulip hybrids of his day, but the pure black tulip he believed he had created was thought to have been lost forever. Imagine: a tulip darker than Queen of the Night!"

"Imagine," I repeated faintly.

"Darker than the Black Parrot!" Chinaberry blinked at me. "Darker even than the Negri, or the Midnight, but with a milky white throat . . . beautiful!"

"Obviously you have strong feelings about these tulips," I began, "but why did you ask me—"

We were at the far door of the greenhouse. "Let's go outside," Chinaberry said, grabbing a jacket from the peg. "I'll show you around the grounds."

Going back out into the spring day was a welcome relief from the humid closeness of the greenhouse. But even I had to take a breath at the sight that lay before me.

Chinaberry explained, pleased with my reaction to the beautifully landscaped gardens that lay between the house and the river. An avenue of topiary boxwoods led to a vast formal garden, which was filled with blooming borders around an elaborate fountain surmounted with a crowing marble rooster. The manicured landscaping covered acres, marching everywhere I looked down toward the river in wild profusion and precision. "This is Water Garden," he said proudly.

A stray blossom blew into the bowl of the bubbling fountain as we walked past. The rooster looked up toward heaven.

It took a lot of Poultry Packers to make a landscape like this, I thought, looking around at the vast gardens. I didn't even recognize most of the plantings, but the sheer size and regimented discipline of the design was impressive. It must have taken an army of gardeners to keep this place in order.

"People think I'm like that fool they see on TV." Chinaberry laughed, as if he had read my thoughts. "After the war I got a loan, went into the chicken business, and worked my butt off so I could have a place like this, where I could have a garden as close to paradise as I could get. I based it on the design of the great French and English gardens I saw in Europe

22

during the war. But I've got to show you the best part."

He led me down the steps of the terrace and across the yard, past the topiaries, the fountain, and the yew alley, toward what appeared at first glance to be a giant boxwood wall.

"When I made my first million I had this dug up shrub by shrub and brought over here from an old manor in England." I followed him through an opening in the hedge. The boxwood was well over six feet tall and neatly trimmed at right angles. Once through the hedge, the big old shrubs were planted in such a way as to create a pathway between them that turned first to the right, then to the left, then to the right again, until we came to a dead end against a wall of hedge. We had no choice but to turn back and take another path.

"It's a labyrinth!" I exclaimed after we had wound in and around and through several paths. I was totally lost, disoriented and surrounded on all sides by small green leaves and that peculiar dog-piss smell of boxwood.

"It's a genuine Elizabethan boxwood maze," Chinaberry said proudly. "Four hundred years old and growing strong. There's a bigger, grander maze on some estate in New York, but this one is better maintained and has more dead ends. You'd better stick with me; I've had guests get lost in here, but I know this maze by heart."

After I turned around and realized that I was surrounded on all sides and totally confused by blank green walls, I did as he suggested. We walked deeper and deeper into the hedges, turning right, then right again, and then, against my own instincts, left, then right again. How could Chinaberry tell where he was? One wall looked like another, only an open turquoise sky above us remained constant. But he marched

23

onward, clearly amused by my increasing confusion.

It may have been the second-best maze in America, but I didn't want to see the first. After what seemed like an hour, but was probably only ten or fifteen minutes, we arrived at the heart of the maze, where a small clearing offered a round marble bench.

"Amazing," I said as I sank gratefully onto the bench.

Chinaberry chuckled at my pun. "It is nice, isn't it? This is one of the reasons I want the gardens to be a museum when I'm gone. I want everyone to come here and say, well, Billy knew what he was doing when it came to gardening. This is what I want to be remembered for. That's what I want you to say," he said matter-of-factly. "You see, I want you to write my obituary."

"Huh?" I asked in my usual brilliant and cutting-edge-witted way. I've had a lot of writing requests in my time. *How do you do a press release? If I tell you the story of my life, you can write it down and we can publish it together and split the profits. Will you read my novel? Can you come do a story on our strawberry festival*? But never a request to write an obituary.

Chinaberry frowned impatiently. "I said, I want you to write my obituary," he repeated crisply. "I'll give you all the information you need, and you write it down in the right style. I know there's a style to these things. How much?" He dug into his pants pocket and withdrew a checkbook. "Name a figure. Now that I'm retired and certain things are happening, I've got all the time and money in the world." He chuckled.

I didn't. I was still too stunned.

"Well, Mr. Chinaberry, when someone's as uh . . . prominent as you are, generally networks and news services and the big papers have already started a file on

24

you, so when you actually *do* die, all they have to do is add the dates and details. For us lesser mortals the undertakers generally write the obit up. Are you by any chance planning on dying, Mr. Chinaberry?" I sensed a story here, even if I hadn't quite caught it on the upstroke.

He shot me a look that should have peeled my paint. But I don't peel easily. This could be a scoop. "I am a rich man, Ms. Ball," he repeated. "I want my obituary done up right. And I pay for what I want, which includes your discretion. Do we have a deal?" His pen poised above the checkbook and he gave me a beady, avian look.

"Sure," I said. *Hey, I'm easy.*

He produced a typed piece of paper. "I had my former secretary write this all down. My family, my college, my four ex-wives, the poultry businesses, Water Garden Museum, all of that. Stress Water Garden, that's the project I want to be remembered for, that and my experiments with flowering bulbs. It's all the information you'll need. When the time comes, you can update it. Can you write it now? I have some unexpected downtime. I hate downtime. Big meeting in Paris tomorrow. I'm still on the board, you know. Selling *poulets* to the *grenouilles*. And I need this done now, before I fly to Europe."

"Sure," I said soothingly. "If you want to go into the study I'll boot up your computer and write it now."

"Let's do it," he said crisply. He rose and offered me his arm, leaning on me slightly as we made our way back to the house.

"That must have been quite something, finding that car at the bottom of the river," he said conversationally as we strolled the grounds like a couple in a Jane Austen novel.

"It was strange to see it come up after all those

25

years," I admitted.

"Your story said it was a red Cadillac Coupe de Ville, didn't it?" he asked.

"One of those old tail-fin jobs. But it had plates from sixty-eight, you could see."

"And there was a body in the car?"

"Bones. A woman's bones, Doc Westmore said when he came. But the ME's office in Baltimore can tell a lot more. It wasn't so much gruesome as sort of sad."

"Was there anything else?"

"Not that I know of. Just the bones, and they weren't in great shape—"

Chinaberry clutched my arm tightly and began to cough. We had to stop while he bent nearly double, his body racked with spasms.

"Are you okay? Should I get the housekeeper?" I asked when he'd recovered himself.

The old man stiffened. "No, no, I'm fine. I just had a bit of a . . . well, never mind! Shall we proceed?" His smile was a rictus, and I knew he was a lot sicker than he was letting on, perhaps even to himself. No wonder he wanted an obituary, I thought.

I took all the information he gave me, and I wrote his obit up in the perfectly standard obituary style you'd see in any newspaper. It took me all of fifteen minutes, while he barked into the telephone in French. It was certainly nothing special; an undertaker could have written it while in a deep coma. "Now that they've found Renata I haven't got much time," he muttered under his breath as he paced the room.

I glanced up at him, but his expression was unreadable. I thought perhaps I'd misunderstood him. Or maybe Renata was some sort of terminal chicken-magnate disease you got from handling too much

26

money. "Huh?" I asked.

Chinaberry waved his hands at me in a shooing gesture. "Please, Ms. Ball, keep typing." He began to read aloud." 'Of all Chinaberry's accomplishments, he was most proud of Water Garden, the proposed arboretum and museum to be housed at his estate of the same name. An amateur breeder, he spent twenty years attempting to hybridize a perfect black tulip.' You can clean that prose up, can't you? Good. Well, type on, type on! I haven't got much time, you know." The twang of his Shore accent still clung to his tones.

While I sat at his monster computer and worked, Chinaberry hovered above me, looking down at the words forming on the screen. From time to time he would nod, grunting his approval or shaking his head at my mistakes. All the while he paced nervously, glancing at his watch. When I'd finished to his satisfaction and given him both a hard copy and a disk, he wrote me a check for five hundred dollars. A personal check.

"I do like your style, Miz Ball," he said, relaxing slightly. "You ought to be writing for the *Sun* or the *Post* instead of that miserable rag the *Gazette.*"

"That's what I think too, but the *Sun* and the *Post* don't seem to think so." I grinned.

"Well, I know a few people. Let me see what I can do," he promised as he showed me out the door, tucking the disk into his pocket.

As I climbed into the car I frowned. Not for the first time since I gave up the noxious weed, I yearned for a cigarette to help me mull this all over.

"Did I hear him say 'Renata'?" Sam—or rather, Sam's ghost—suddenly appeared, sprawled on the passenger seat.

"How long have you been lurking around?" I

27

demanded. "You know I hate it when you lurk and I don't know you're there."

Sam frowned. "I heard him say 'Renata.' That was the only reason why I showed up here. For your information, I *do* have a life."

"Which the Rules prohibit you from discussing with me—"

"The point is, what did he say about Renata?" Sam cut me off impatiently.

"I don't know. He muttered something about how they found Renata and not having a lot of time. Is that some kind of terminal thing?"

He sighed, shaking his head. "And you call yourself a reporter."

The car phone rang. Its shrill tone startled us both. I had forgotten that the paper had issued me one, because I wasn't allowed to use it for outgoing calls and to rack up bills against the owner's cash cow.

"That," Sam said, "will be that cop pal of yours, Friendly."

"Ormand's not my 'cop pal,' he's my—"

What was he? Before I had to answer that, I'd located the damned phone beneath a pile of half-read newspapers in the backseat.

"Hollis? I called the *Gazette,* but they said you were probably out covering a story," a familiar voice barked.

"He's going to tell you that the corpse in the Cadillac they pulled out of the river yesterday has just been identified as Renata Ringwood Clinton." Sam settled back in the seat and smiled.

"How do you know this stuff?" I asked my ghost.

"How do I know what stuff?" Friendly grunted on the other end of the phone. "They traced the registration number through the DMV. How did you know that's what

I was calling about? Look, I need a local's perspective, and since you're my favorite local I'm starting with you. It's about that skeleton they found in the Caddy. We think, after we ID'd the car, that it might be a woman named Renata Ringwood Clinton. She disappeared from Beddoe's Island around sixty-eight or so."

"Renata Clinton?" I repeated stupidly.

Sam just smiled. He didn't even bother to open his eyes. *Now that they've found Renata I haven't got much time,* Billy Chinaberry had muttered to himself.

Renata wasn't a disease, it was a recovered corpse.

". . . it'll take the medical examiner's office a while to confirm it; they're going to track down her dental records. After almost thirty years underwater, all that was left of her was those bones," Friendly continued cheerfully. "But you saw all that, right?"

"I caught a glimpse when you law types weren't blocking the view," I replied. The craving for nicotine passed over me again, and I rubbed the patch on my shoulder as if that would help.

"Look, Hollis, if this is Renata Ringwood Clinton from Beddoe's Island we got here, hon, what do you know, off the record and the top of your head?"

Flashback time. "Big, big black bouffant hair," I said immediately. "I mean big. Like Marie Antoinette hair, only it was all teased and sprayed and towering. I was about five or six then, but I still thought it was incredibly cool. She looked like Priscilla Presley in the wedding photos."

Sam made a circle of his thumb and forefinger.

"Well," Friendly said doubtfully, "There wasn't a whole lotta hair left . . . ."

But I was back in my childhood, remembering Miss Renata. Wow, was that a while ago or what? "She was

29

my friend Jenny's mom. She was really different from the other women on the island. I mean, she wasn't like a mom was supposed to be. She wore these tight bell bottoms and halter tops and a lot of makeup and big jewelry and stuff . . ." God, it was all coming back to me in a rush now. Even as a small child I had been impressed by Mrs. Renata Clinton. "You just don't forget a towering mass of matte-black dyed hair like she had. Of course, massive, teased bouffant hair was the fashion then, but hers must have had its own zip code," I recalled. "Then she and Busbee got a divorce, and she and Jennifer moved somewhere else and I never saw them again. Jennifer Clinton was my best friend when I was a little kid, so I played at their house a lot."

"What else do you remember?" Friendly asked impatiently.

I shook my head. "You should really call my mom. Miss Dolly and her friends would probably tell you all about her. I was just a little kid. I don't remember too much, except there was this big mess around the divorce, but it was grown-up stuff so we kids didn't hear much about it."

I could almost see Friendly writing this all down. It was on the tip of my tongue to tell him where I was calling from, but I thought about how that check could buy the Honda the new tires and two new *C V* boots it desperately needed that I couldn't afford on a small-town reporter's salary.

"Okay, hon, will do. They estimate she's been down there for about thirty years. She was reported missing January thirteenth, 1968. There was a big snow and ice storm on the twelfth. They surmised she was driving across the old Calais Road Bridge when it was coated with ice, and the car just slid off the road and went into the water. Just disappeared like that. It seems strange, but I found a similar case on the net about a vanload of kids who went into a canal in South Florida and weren't found for fifteen years. Hell of a way to go, isn't it?"

"Bridge freezes before road surface," I quoted, and tried not to think about it too much. It was a slow, ugly way to die, trapped in a car under the water.

Friendly sighed, changing the mood. "Listen, hon, this is off the record, okay? I'll have the official confirm on Monday. Wanna meet me at the Horny Mallard for lunch?"

He was about to say more interesting things about him and me, but I heard his pager go off, so I agreed to lunch and rang off. I knew this case was going to keep him on the go for the immediate future, which might rule out our weekend plans. If it wasn't my work, it was his. "The only way I ever get to see him is if someone gets killed," I sighed.

Sam snorted in disgust and changed the subject. "The last time I saw Billy Chinaberry I was still alive. He's a pal of my father's in the Eastern-Shore-Billionaire-Boys'-Club sort of way the really rich stick together. War buddies or something. At least that's settled," he added, but it never occurred to me to ask him what he meant.

"You know what I think? I think you have too much time on your hands, and—"

But my spirit ex-husband had disappeared as suddenly as he had arrived.

"Men!" I sighed.

Well, I deposited the check, got my cousin Larry to repair the Honda, and wrote up the discovery, when it was officially announced that the corpse in the Coupe de Ville was Renata Ringwood Clinton.

This caused a mild stir, then was forgotten in the big

flap when Chuckles La Roma the Albino Clown, jumped off the Bay Bridge after he was denied tenure at Santimoke College. Chuckles was the first Eva Gabor Chair in Entertainment Studies to suicide off the westbound span, so you can just imagine what it was like to write that up.

But in my line you get a lot of weird incidents, things that happen where you never learn the ending. Billy Chinaberry's connection to Renata Ringwood, I thought, was one of those open-ended tales. Unlike the tale of Chuckles, whose tenure had been denied because billing himself as the Albino Clown was considered politically incorrect by the Faculty Review Committee. They wanted him to use Pigmentally Impaired.

Sam, wherever he was, made no further appearances for a while. I suppose he does have a real life (?) somewhere else, although I've never been able to discover precisely what that might entail.

I had not one clue how many ugly things Renata Ringwood Clinton brought up with her from thirty years on the bottom of the river.

But I would. Oh, but I would.

CHAPTER 4

IT'S HARD TO BE RELIGIOUS WHEN CERTAIN PEOPLE ARE NEVER INCINERATED BY BOLTS OF LIGHTNING

EVERY ONCE IN A WHILE I ALLOW MY MOTHER TO DRAG me off to the 10:00 A.M. Sunday service at Beddoe's Island United Methodist Church. That there will be Sunday dinner afterward may or may not be a bribe, depending on whether or not you have ever tasted Dolly Ball's cooking. When tourists come to the island and ask me where they can get a good meal, I tell them at my mother's house. I'm cruel that way. But until you put your legs under Miss Doll's table, you don't know what good Eastern Shore cooking is.

This being April and the shadbush in bloom, there would be herring roe on the table. I am very partial to herring roe the way my mother does it, rolled in cornmeal and deep-fried to a golden crisp, cholesterol be damned. Served with new watercress and some of her tomato relish, it's the closest thing to heaven on this planet. So what if you can't eat anything but vegetables for the rest of the week?

If my thoughts were straying away from the Reverend Linda Tate's sermon, drifting toward the idea of biting into those firm, round herring eggs, you can understand why.

The District Supervisor had sent Beddoe's Island the gift of Ms. Tate about a year ago, and as far as I was concerned the earnest young minister was a tad too far on the Wesleyan side. Since she was about my age, I think I had expected her to be a shade more liberal. Maybe I was fooled by the ponytail and the wire-rim glasses that made her look like the late Jerry Garcia. I'm not being bitchy; she really did have the look of a Deadhead who had somehow gotten lost on the way to the next concert and ended up in the ministry.

But my tastes have changed since I moved away from Beddoe's Island, where they like their religion hard-shell and their law enforcement soft-shell. Apparently the island liked Ms. Tate just fine, judging from the sound of someone signifying loudly behind us.

"Let us pray for the sinner and the lost! Sinners, come

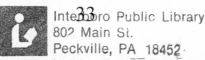

to Jesus!" Ms. Tate exhorted.

"Amen!"

This came from the biggest sinner in Beddoe's Island. Signifying in church nailed another one of Busbee Clinton's many transgressions. On Sunday he was the loudest, most public Methodist you'd ever want to hear. The rest of the week he spent his time studying on new and better ways to screw his fellow Christians. He would have cheerfully screwed Buddhists, Muslims, Jews, and Santerians too, if there were any around, so no one needed to feel as if they were left out of Busbee's agenda. He was a multicultural, equal-opportunity screwer-over.

If someone tells you what a Christian they are, turn and run the other way. It seems to me that the real Christians—or Muslims, Buddhists, Jews, and Santerians—are the ones who lead their lives quietly and steadily, putting their faith into daily practice, not public display on high holy days.

"Praise Jay-*zus*!" Busbee sang out, loud and clear. As Beddoe's Island's richest man and owner of Clinton's Seafood, where most of the watermen sold their catch and a lot of the women used to work for minimum wage before the tool factory opened in Watertown, Busbee had had many chances to offend everyone. And Busbee was not a man to miss a chance.

"Goddamned sumbitch," my father said under his breath. I wondered what was Busbee's latest transgression. Since my father is president of the Beddoe's Island Waterman's Association, I figured it had something to do with the seafood buyers' dealings. My mother frowned, torn between shock at his expressing himself thus in church and agreement with his assessment of Busbee.

34

"Hypocrite," my brother Robbie muttered from the other side of Dad. There was a chorus of low rumblings from around the congregation, mostly from watermen and their families.

Callie, my sister-in-law, shot Robbie a dirty look, but didn't say anything, probably because she agreed with him. My mother sniffed loudly, fanning herself with the church bulletin.

Little Miss Rosanne Buck, the organist, looked out at us as if she thought we were beyond salvation, that we were all speeding on Route 666, the highway to hell. She peered over her glasses at me and I waved. She once told me I was a godless liberal media person, hinting at a dark future in the afterlife. Seeing my wave, Miss Rosanne hurriedly returned to her sheet music.

Was it just my imagination running away with me, or was something really interesting going on around here? Since I no longer lived on the island, I was not always au courant with the latest developments. But my reporter sense was twitching.

"We have sinned, but through Grace we are redeemed," Reverend Tate announced.

"Oh, yas, praise Jay-*zus*!"

I turned to glance at Busbee a few pews behind us. With his greasy gray pompadour and his up-in-your-face plaid sport jacket, he looked as if he'd dropped out of a fifties time capsule over Las Vegas. His beringed hands were clasped just below his string tie, and his eyes were firmly raised to heaven, the very portrait of piety.

Did I say *be-ringed?* The man looked as if he'd been hitting Elvis's yard sales. Diamond and onyx stones studded the heavy gold lumps on his fingers; thick gold chains dangling with figas, nuggets, crosses, and anchors nestled in the screaming yellow polyester shirtfront beneath his wattled neck.

"Praise Jay-*zus*!"

The richest man on Beddoe's Island and owner of Clinton's Seafood had a certain reputation for pure meanness—both fiscal and spiritual—that must have taken some effort to uphold. In short, he was considered as tight as a tick and as venomous as a snake. I wondered again what he'd done to stir up the island against him this time.

"Turn around," Mom hissed at me.

I did.

"Before the benediction," Linda Tate was saying, "let us take a brief moment to pray for the soul of Renata Ringwood Clinton, whose body was tragically recovered at Calais Bridge last week. As some of you may have noticed, we are able to welcome Renata and Busbee Clinton's daughter Jennifer today. We have a genuine celebrity among us."

While most people dutifully bent their heads for a moment of silence, the curious among us turned to stare.

Busbee's sharp, vulpine features were still screwed into a public expression of devotion, and I could smell his heavy, slightly stale cologne three pews away, but I was looking at the woman seated beside him.

The hair was bright honey gold instead of brown, the aquiline Clinton nose had been reshaped, and thirty-odd years had done its work on us all, but it was Jennifer all right. She stared straight ahead, her expression bemused, as if she were not quite certain what she was doing in a country church in a Chesapeake Bay backwater.

When we were kids she had been my best friend. We played together nearly every day. After the divorce,

36

when Jen and Renata had left the island for New York, we'd written back and forth for a while, but kids being kids, that had trickled off long before we reached puberty.

In the past couple of years, however, I had been able to keep up with my childhood friend's career through my mother, whose weekday schedule revolved around *Hapless Hearts,* the soap opera where Jennifer Clinton played Carla Devane, the scheming town vixen of Payne Valley. When last heard from, supermodel/ psychiatrist Carla had been kidnapped by Stud, her fifth or sixth ex-husband, and held captive in his isolated mountain stronghold while he tried to prevent her from recuperating from her bout of amnesia, lest she recall that she had divorced Clete and that Ava had had a child by Stud, who would inherit everything if Wanda didn't survive the big operation, which she wouldn't if Todd kept performing surgery while he was drugged up on prescription painkillers. All the men on *Hapless Hearts* were fools in love with Carla.

It seemed to me that most of the people on the island were also in love with her. Being on a soap opera had made Jen a hometown heroine in these parts, where a lot of people watch daytime TV—especially the watermen, whose days start at 3:00 A.M. and end just about in time to come home, shuck out of their boots, pop open a cold one, and check out the soaps.

"Is that really Jen Clinton? When did she come back here?" I asked my mother out of the side of my mouth.

"When the avalanche that Crystal started when she shot Piers buried Stud's isolated mountain stronghold," Mom replied, looking straight ahead. I studied her profile long enough to decide she was talking about the character Jennifer played on the soap, not my childhood friend, and went back to counting the flowers on the altar until Miss Rosanne struck up the opening chords of "God Will Take Care of You." God had better; some of us can't find our own behinds with two hands, a native guide, and a road map.

"What brings her back here?" I whispered as we struggled with the hymnbook.

Mom pursed her lips, torn between giving me the latest gossip and reprimanding me for my lack of church manners. "They say Busbee's thinking about changing his will." She cast me a look. "I think he's probably figured out a way to take it all with him."

We both giggled at that, and I knew I was forgiven as we said the benediction. From the interior of her vast purse Mom withdrew a plastic grocery sack. My mother is nothing if not prepared for all events. "Whyn't you nip around back of Aunt Lucille's and pick some 'spargus for dinner?" she asked me as we shuffled out of the pew. "Since Aunty went to visit your cousin Mary Ellen up to Seaford, it's just settin' there goin' to sprout. You can go 'round the back way through the fellowship hall and avoid the minister's line."

As I left the church a thin April sunlight shone down on my head, and I gratefully inhaled the loamy smell of green and emerging spring. Washed clean by spring showers and bathed in a clear Edward Hopper light, the village of Beddoe's Island looked deceptively tranquil. Narrow streets of neatly made frame houses were shaded by budding trees and framed by distant views of bright blue water and pale blue sky. The old graveyard behind the church was dotted with Easter flowers from the past Sunday's service. I picked my way through the thin white headstones of my ancestors across the painfully green grass.

38

If you didn't know better, you'd think Beddoe's Island was a nice, peaceful place.

I know better.

"Holly! Holly Ball!"

When I heard my name being called I turned, and to my great astonishment I saw Jennifer Clinton making her way through the stones, wobbling on her high heels as they sank in the damp earth. "Wait up!" she called, stopping to lean on a stone as she slipped her shoes off, then ran in her stocking feet across the grass toward me.

"Oh, I can't believe it's really you! You haven't changed a bit!" she exclaimed in a throaty, actressy voice as she held me at arm's length for examination. I had the feeling a split second was all it took to appraise every stitch I was wearing and know its price and provenance. The appraising look was gone as quickly as it had come, but I had seen it and I was wary.

Jennifer was all smiles now. "Well, of course, you've changed! You're all grown up, and is that a Liz Claiborne jacket? Listen to me!" she trilled. "But clothes are such a part of the industry that I'm always interested in things I like!"

For my part, I assessed her too. Up close her makeup was just a shade too heavy-handed; she was wearing false eyelashes, of all the known vanities! But there was no denying that she was a beautiful woman; even I could see that.

"It really is you, then, on *Hapless Hearts?* When Mom said that was you, I didn't believe her at first!"

Jen shook her head. "Isn't it a hoot? Four years as a drama major and I end up on daytime TV! Actually, it's unbelievably good exposure for an actress, and I did get those two Emmys." She was pleased, I could tell. Most celebrities are when you recognize them. Isn't that the whole point of fame? More than that, she was pleased with herself. "Remember all the times we used to play dress-up?" she asked.

"With your mother's clothes!" I exclaimed. "She had the most wonderful clothes—"

Jennifer's expression caved in a little.

"Oh, I'm sorry," I said quickly.

She shrugged. "It's just a relief to know where she is! You know, she just disappeared, and for years and years I thought she'd deserted me. Just run off and left me, the way she left Father. When Father called and told me that they'd found her, I felt a huge sense of relief. Now my therapist says I can have some closure." She reached into her bag and extracted a familiar red and white tin Altoids box. "This is the only thing I'm allowed to eat since I stopped smoking," she sighed.

"You too?" I laughed.

Jen nodded ruefully. "I'm on the patch, gum, you name it. God, this is so tough, even tougher than doing the Scottish play!" She offered me the box and popped a mint into her mouth. "I can't afford to gain weight," she sighed complacently.

"Been there, done that, have the T-shirt," I agreed, even though I somehow felt as if she had just told me I was ballooning up. I was tempted to retaliate by telling Jen about being there when they brought her mother up from the bottom of the river, but for once I suppressed the urge. Jen was a grown-up stranger to me; would knowing the gory details help her or upset her? Nonetheless, my professional curiosity was aroused. "So why did you come back?" I asked bluntly.

"I want to know what happened to Mother," she said flatly, meeting my gaze.

"What does Busbee say?"

Jen gave me an oblique look. "About as little as my grandparents. I sort of expected that after all these years he'd at least be interested in seeing me, but it's as if we're strangers. Which I guess we almost are." A perfect teardrop formed in the corner of her eye and hung on her false eyelash, glittering mournfully. "Your mother said you are a reporter now."

I nodded cautiously. "Well, I normally don't do celebrity interviews, but—"

"A crime reporter," Jen persisted. "She says you've won awards. That you really get involved in your work."

"Well . . ." I murmured modestly. That Maryland-Delaware Press Association Award couldn't hold up against two Emmys. But Jen had gripped my arm with all the strength of the withdrawing nicotine addict.

"Your mother said you could help me find out who killed my mother," Jen said in a rush. "Holly, you've got to help me find out who killed her—"

"My mother promised you?" I sighed. *Oh, Mom, not again.* "Jen, it's perfectly normal to think foul play is involved when a person we love is involved in a fatal accident. It's a way of denying that what happened has happened. In my experience there's maybe one time in a thousand when an accidental death is anything other than a tragic, senseless accident." It was a good, prepackaged speech, and usually it worked. "I was there when they retrieved your mother's car from the river, and it was definitely an accident, believe me. The police and the Medical Examiner investigated it thoroughly, and they ruled it an accidental death."

"Jennifer! Jennifer Clinton! Come on along, girl! There's folks waitin' to meet you!" a familiar voice called impatiently.

41

We both looked up to see Busbee Clinton standing beside the church, frowning at us, as in days of old. It seemed to me that Busbee had always been dragging Jen away when we were kids. Evidently, that much hadn't changed.

"I knew you'd help me," Jennifer said in that breathless actress voice, as if I hadn't just said no. She smiled and shrugged. "I've got an obligation to my public," she said, and I realized she was completely serious. "I'll be in touch soon!" she breathed as she air-kissed my cheek.

Jen slipped her high-heeled pumps back on and tripped gracefully through the tombstones, back toward her father and her public.

Busbee glared at me for a second, then turned to follow his daughter.

There were these two old metal soda fountain chairs that lived in the cemetery behind the church. They'd been around as long as anyone could remember. Doll used to say that they had been there when she was a girl, and Hollis's late grandmother used to say she couldn't remember a time when those two chairs weren't there, winter and summer, just sitting among the headstones. Hollis once told me the kids called them the Devil's Chairs and dared each other to sit in them, convinced that to sit in them was to descend—probably through some trapdoor—directly into hell.

Lots of things "disappeared" around the island, but never those two chairs. Not even the least superstitious person (rational is not a word I use in connection with Beddoe's Island) would have dreamed of stealing the Devil's Chairs.

But here we were, invisible to the living, sitting in

them, and our spirits had not descended into a fiery netherworld.

"Was that really Carla Devane?" I asked, agog.

"Don't tell me you're a fan too." Renata laughed indulgently.

"Wouldn't miss an episode of Hapless Hearts. When Stud held Carla prisoner in his isolated mountain cabin, I was on the edge of my seat. I still don't know what's happening, except Todd's popping pills and performing brain surgery on Wanda—"

"Please!" She held up both hands.

"Hollis better get a hustle on that asparagus, because her mother just set the herring roe under the broiler."

We watched as Hollis walked, oblivious, through the half-formed ether of an unformed spirit haunting its own headstone. Since it was more ectoplasm than intelligence, as such spirits are, it did not note her passing. The unseen world is full of such revenants, half-formed and powerless creatures, little more than amoebas, shades of their former living intelligence, in transition from one world to the next.

Renata sighed, moving restlessly, looking past me toward her daughter. Her expression was wistful. "My Jennifer grew up to be a real beauty, didn't she?" the dark-haired woman asked, twisting the bracelets on her wrist.

"Indeed she did," I agreed. "She's a beautiful woman." Renata, I sensed, had probably been a beautiful woman too, invested with all the power the living accord to those who possess great comeliness. And I saw, with the awful hindsight of the dead, where that beauty had gotten her.

"All those lost years," Renata murmured. "So cold down there, so wet, and my girl growing up without me,

Sam."

I said nothing. What could I say? What can any of us, the dead, say about those we left behind? Our times of living were unfinished canvases, shadowy sketches of sadness, of what might have been.

Renata and I sat together in silence—in this world, but not of it—and the spring breeze, crisp with the smell of the river and of blooming things, stirred through us. It was one of those mornings. when I missed the mortal coil.

She sighed again. "It's not for me." She repeated, "It's really not for me. It's for her, you know." Her bangles jangled on her arms like the song of birds only I could hear.

"I'm doing the best I can," I replied.

"If only they could see me!" Renata fretted "If I just knew who did it!"

CHAPTER 5

FAMILY VALUES

"MOM, I WISH YOU WOULDN'T TELL PEOPLE I'LL investigate it every time they think they see a scandal or a cover-up. For one thing I'm *not* an investigative reporter, and for another your friends are so paranoid and crazy that they see scandals and cover-ups under every bushel basket." I waved a forkload of herring roe in my mother's direction. "I don't have time to indulge some drama-queen soap diva! There was nothing suspicious about the way Miss Renata died. It was an accident!"

"Holly, ask your father if he remembered to pick up

44

the tomato sets when he went to Southern States," my mother said, passing Callie the biscuits.

I sighed, then turned to my father. "Well?" I asked. "Did you?"

My father raised his busby eyebrows. "Did I what?" he asked me, all innocence, as if he hadn't heard.

Robbie chewed silently, avoiding eye contact, but Callie, reaching for the butter, glared at me warningly.

"This is really stupid, you know," I pointed out.

"Don't be disrespectful to your mother, Holly," my father said.

"Mother wants to know if you picked up the tomato sets from Southern States." I sighed. Sunday dinner with Perk and Doll can reduce me to the level of a truculent fourteen-year-old all over again.

"Tell your mother that I bought six Beef Boys and two Romas," Dad told me. "They said they'd have them Hungarian peppers next week. Ask your mother if she thinks we ought to set out the 'loupes this week."

I dutifully turned to my mother. "Mom, Dad wants to know if you think you should set out the cantaloupes this week."

My mother dabbed her lips with her napkin. "Tell your father I set them out last week, which he would know if he took the least interest in what's going on around his own home instead of hanging around down doing Waterman's Association business instead of his own all the time."

"I refuse to repeat that," I said.

"Hollis Louisa Ball, do I have to tell you twice to be respectful of your mother?" my father demanded. He spooned watercress salad into his plate, spilling some on his good Sunday tie.

"Mom says you spend too much time down to the

45

Association meetings," I told him.

"Maybe if some of the women on this island spent less time down to the Methodist Women Rummage Sale Committee and more time at home where they belong, this house would be a better place to live," my father said.

Callie leaned across the table and smiled at me. "Mr. Perk has called for a watermen's strike," she translated.

"Holly, will you tell my wife not to torment my father about what is no one else's bidness?" Robbie asked me, glaring at Callie.

"Holly, will you tell my husband—"

"That's enough!" I exclaimed, picking up my plate. "I've had it! My food's getting cold! If you all want to argue, you don't need me to do it!" I got up and walked into the kitchen, where my niece and nephew were eating at that remarkable Sunday and high-holy-day institution, the kids' table.

"You're too old to eat with us," Jason told me in his not-quite-a-baby lisp.

"If you weren't so cute you'd be dead," I told him.

"Oh, be quiet," Megan loftily commanded him. "Aunt Holly can eat wherever she wants to. Do *you* want to eat with *them?*"

Jason shook his head so hard that his red hair—the same color as his mother's—swung from side to side.

"They've been making us talk for them all week," Megan informed me with all the world-weariness of ten-going-on-thirty. "I'm really sick of it, and so is Jason."

"Tell them they're traumatizing you," I advised. "Tell them that all this stupid bickering is interfering with your early-childhood development and you're both going to grow up to become ax murderers."

"I heard that!" Robbie called from the dining room.

46

"Stop teaching my kids to act smart. This idnit one o' those soap operas!"

"It's my duty as their aunt to make sure they carry on the tradition," I called back through the open doorway. To Megan I said, "Repeat after me: 'Ax murderer.' 'Traumatic events in early childhood.' "

"You're silly," she informed me, wrinkling her nose.

"And you are too smart for your years," I replied loftily before we both broke into giggles.

I lifted a forkful of beautiful, golden crisp herring roe to my mouth. It was cold. Doubtless it had had a chance to cool down while I was interpreting for the warring factions. No good deed goes unpunished.

Sighing, I rose and put my plate into the microwave on the counter.

"Well, Perk, it's not your fault," Mom was saying in the dining room, emotion evidently overruling her vow of spousal silence. "It's that son of a bitch Busbee Clinton!" Since my mother disapproves of bad language, this was nearly unprecedented.

"Miss Doll is right!" Callie chimed in, falling right behind her in the marital arts. "I don't know why we're all fighting among ourselves when it's that rat who's caused all the trouble!"

"You're right, Callie, just as right as can be, honey," my brother said. I figured he would finally get some that night. "It's Busbee Clinton we need to fight!"

"First it was the crab pickin' and now it's drivin' out the other buyers!" my father said angrily.

From the dining room there was suddenly animated discussion, punctuated only by the clink of silver against ceramic. From what I could gather, Busbee Clinton had somehow chased away the island's other two crab buyers, leaving Clinton's Seafood as the only outlet available to an island waterman who wished to sell his crabs. Unless he wanted to off-load his catch from his boat, move it into the back of his pickup truck and drive twenty miles to Watertown, Busbee Clinton—and his low prices paid—was now the only game on the island.

As a consequence my father, president of the Beddoe's Island Watermen's Association, had called a strike, and no one was crabbing at all. Their boats had lain idle in the cove all week. And now the Beddoe's Island women were mad at the men. Since most of the ladies already worked full-time, raised kids, and kept house while the men lurked around the general store and Toby's Bar, muttering like extras in a bad play about the French Revolution, I could understand their anger. I suppose when the men came home and started to use their free time to advise their wives on how to cook, clean, and budget the diminished income, quite a few of the striking watermen found out just how things really stood.

Only Karl Marx could have been happier than I was that they'd finally identified their common enemy as the capitalist oppressor Busbee Clinton. I've always been a closet lefty, especially when Busbee is the running-dog lackey of the decadent free-market system.

"Watermen of the world, unite! You have nothing to lose but your trotlines!" I called out.

"I won't have that communis' talk in my house," my father pronounced from the dining room.

"Especially not in front of the grandchildren!" my mother agreed.

"Can you say 'hard-line Maoist'?" I whispered to the next generation.

While we were laughing milk out of our noses, the

party meeting in the dining room raged on, and Busbee Clinton was getting more carved up than the herring roe.

This wasn't the first of Busbee's many transgressions against the island, just the latest. When I was a kid the women of Beddoe's Island made a living from the crabs their husbands caught; they steamed and picked out the meat in their own kitchens. In those days, when most women on the island dropped out of high school to get married and were soon enough stuck at home with small children to raise, a cottage industry like crab picking was a valuable part of the family's total income. I could recall watching my own mother's hands flying with her short, sharp knife as the white meat piled up on the kitchen table and the spicy aroma of bay leaves filled the house on early summer mornings. Like most island women, Mom got up all summer at 3:00 A.M. with Dad, steaming her crabs in a vast pot during the cooler morning before dawn. By the time Robbie and I were awake she was generally cleaning up, her neatly filled metal cans lining their own refrigerator on the back porch, waiting for the wholesaler to come and fetch them away.

Then one day, when I was Megan's age, the state-health-department people were coming around, declaring the kitchens of Beddoe's Island housewives unsanitary and their practice of dumping the shells overboard unhealthful to the Bay.

It's hard for an outsider to imagine which accusation made the islanders more indignant: that crab shells and crab leavings were polluting the same Chesapeake Bay from which they'd come, or that a Beddoe's Island woman's kitchen was anything less than clean enough to eat off the floor. Nor had there been any complaints about bad seafood from the restaurants and wholesalers, who prized Beddoe's Island crabmeat for its quality and lack of shell fragments.

All of a sudden the women were being threatened with fines and jail for doing what they'd done for a hundred years. Then Busbee Clinton built his state-approved, stainless-steel-equipped packing house and offered the women jobs at about half of what they'd been making at home. Most folks got the idea that Busbee, who enjoyed hobnobbing with the big state boys, had screwed over his fellow islanders once again. But the women had gone to work for him. What choice did they have?

"I don't want you to ever have to pick crabs for a living," my mother had said more than once when she came home exhausted from eight hours on her feet, shoving the fives and tens into the cookie jar. Those fives and tens paid for a lot of my college.

These days I had to hand that much to the growth of the industry and tourism in the county: An uneducated woman could get a minimum-wage job waiting tables or cleaning rooms or working at the tool factory in Watertown and tell Busbee to go screw himself.

In the first flush of tourists Mom became the head cook at the Island Light Restaurant, and she had made pretty good money. I'd waitressed there through college, along with Callie. My sister-in-law—smart girl that she is—got herself an R.N. and worked up at the Watertown Hospital. Her folks, like mine, were determined that we would never pick a crab for Busbee Clinton.

Eventually, he'd shut down his packing house and started shipping his crabs to Watertown, where they were picked by the Latina women who came from Mexico and Nicaragua and Guatemala to join their husbands, men who labored in Bill Chinaberry's chicken-processing plants. Jobs no one else around here wanted—not when going on welfare paid more.

I knew what my parents had sacrificed to put me through school, and I knew that they were often disappointed that I'd used my college education to end up on the local paper, when they'd hoped I'd go into a respectable occupation like Callie had. The fact that my marriage had turned out to be a disaster hadn't helped much either. I was supposed to be the bright one in the family, but sometimes my parents clearly wondered about my choices. At least no one had mentioned my lack of a second marriage or my production of grandchildren today. But the afternoon was young.

Actually, I brooded, since I'd started going around with Ormand Friendly they'd been a little more tight-lipped on that subject. As respectable Beddoe's Islanders they of course deplored government, especially law enforcement. But on the other hand they liked Friendly—possibly a whole lot more than I did at that point. Somehow he'd managed to ingratiate himself with my family in ways I never could. And I was holding that against him.

"Dysfunctional family reunion," I muttered to myself. "Everyone brings a covered dish and an unresolved issue." It didn't make my guilt go away, but it did quiet it down a little. I took another bite of my roe. It was still cold. With a sigh I rose and went back to the microwave.

I pushed in the button, and the nuke hummed to half-life. While I waited for it to do its thing, I stared out the window above the sink. I had a fine view across the backyard and down into the harbor, where the idle workboats and skipjacks rode at mooring in the Sunday sunlight. I blinked at the shiny black car that had been rolled up among the pickup trucks. Pleasure cars were rarely to be found in Shadbush Cove, and this one was shiny and expensive-looking. There seemed to be only one person aboard, a lanky individual who looked to be hovering nervously over the steering wheel. Tourist, I thought. Otherwise, the harbor was as quiet as a Sunday morning at Toby's Bar. I tried to figure out the make of the car, but it was impossible at that distance, given what I know about cars, which is very little.

As I was contemplating this unfamiliar sight I was somewhat surprised to see Busbee Clinton's purple Eldorado pull up at the docks. "Speak of the capitalist oppressor!" I exclaimed.

"You mind your manners, miss!" my niece said to me in an uncanny imitation of my father.

"Show some respect," Jason echoed wisely, smearing sweet potato all over himself in an effort to get some into his mouth.

I had to laugh. "Say 'talk-show trash,' kids," I instructed them.

"Don't teach them those words," Robbie called from the dining room. "You're a bad influence on them, Holly. I've had complaints from their teachers. They know it's your work, especially Mrs. Snelgrove."

When I looked again the Eldorado was pulling off in a cloud of dust, and the black car was still sitting there. I couldn't make out the driver.

Just then the timer on the nuke dinged, and my attention was focused squarely on food again.

The afternoon ended pretty much as it always did, with Dad and Robbie drowsing in front of ESPN on the TV, and Mom and Callie in the kitchen doing the dishes. My job was to play with the kids, so we bundled on our jackets and took a stroll around the yard while I disseminated nature information, some of which was even accurate.

We examined Dad's squirrel chair, refilled the bird feeders, and poked at a dead rat with a stick. It was disintegrating nicely, thank you, since the last time we'd looked. All in all a fine spring afternoon.

We were shaking out the apple tree's new blossoms—a nice sort of *Wind in the* Willows kid thing to do—when Busbee Clinton rode up into the drive and tapped right smart on the horn of the Eldorado.

His usual grayish pallor was suffused with a dark red, and his little red-veined eyes were snapping with anger behind his glasses as he leaned out of the window and snarled at me. "Is your father around? Where is he?" Busbee opened the car door, stuck one skinny leg out, and then all hell broke loose. I noticed that he was wearing only a bathrobe and that flecks of soap were still stuck to his many gold necklaces, as if he had been interrupted in his toilette. The sight of Busbee Clinton in a bathrobe was not something I would have paid to see. The man had skinny white toothpick legs and horny yellow toenails.

My father flew out of the house in his stocking feet as if cued by an offstage prompter, and he looked as if he could spit nails. He was pumping his .12 gauge as he came through the door. My brother was right behind him, carrying his old high-school baseball bat, his face white with fury.

Mom and Callie were not far behind. Mom had a kitchen knife in one hand and the cordless phone in the other, while Callie was pushing a shell into Dad's .28 gauge Handy pistol.

My family at home.

It was quite the *tableau vivant.*

The kids and I stood stock-still under the apple tree, eyes as wide as saucers. This was not the sort of behavior that the Steamboat Road Balls—unlike some people on this island I could mention—indulged in, and I was acutely aware that the neighbors were emerging from their homes to see what was happening and whether or not they should participate. The fact that most of the men were out of work added an extra *je ne sais quoi* to their interest. Talk about people with too much time on their hands.

"Now, see here, Perk, you got no call to do this!" Busbee said, his Adam's apple bobbing up and down as he hopped from one bare foot to the other, struggling to keep his bathrobe modestly closed.

"I told you if I saw your sorry ass on my property, I'd blow you back through the bulkheads, Busbee, and I meant what I said!" Dad, usually the most mild of men, growled. "Doll, call the po-lice."

"I got 911 on the line, Perk," my mother said grimly, swelling with righteous indignation and the determination of a mother lioness protecting her young.

"Don't you make a move, Busbee," Robbie said thickly. "Keep your hands out where we can see 'em."

"You as much as *look* at my family, you old devil, I'll rip your spine out and beat you to death with it," Mom hissed, truly magnificent.

"I ain't moving nowhere," Busbee said in a quavering voice. Since he was standing barefoot on our oyster-shell driveway, this posture could not have been easy to maintain, but I guess it beat a faceful of buckshot. "Iffen you called me over here so's you could murder me in cold blood, Perky Ball, then you're a bigger fool than I thought you was." His gold chains glittered in the sunlight.

My father frowned. "I didn't call *you*, you old fool! You just called *me* on the phone!"

"Like hell I did! You called me! My daughter was there; she'll tell the world that I just hung up on your sorry behind!" Realizing he had been steadily drawing an audience from all over the neighborhood, Busbee sniffled, looking around uneasily. "You just called me up and told me if I didn't give you damned watermen your goddamned price on crabs, you was gonna blow me back through the bulkheads! As Gawd's my witness I never shortchanged no one in my whole life!" His whine was that of a cornered miser in a bad Dickens novel.

I wasn't the only one looking skyward for a bolt of lightning to strike him. From the Swaynes' porch next door I heard Ellery give a distinct snort and Mertis gasp, taking it all in. Out of the corner of my eye I could see our other neighbors gathering, angry watermen and their angrier wives standing just outside the range of the guns. They looked as if they were just curious, but with the mood against Busbee Clinton on the island that day, they could just as easily have turned into an angry mob.

Even *I* didn't find the idea of lynching Busbee all that unappealing, and *I* disliked the man just on general principals.

"Be that as it may, Busbee Clinton," my mother was saying, "you can't set on our property and say you didn't just call up here not five minutes ago and threaten to kill Perk for gettin' the Watermen's Association all stirred up against you!" She took a deep breath and crossed her hands over her bosom. "Don't say you didn't neither, because you were yelling so loud I could hear you all the way to the kitchen!"

"Did not!" Busbee cried. "I don't know what you are up to this time, but I'll tell the world we was settin' down to watch the O's play Cleveland, an' the phone rings and it's you, Perky Ball, a-whoppin' and a-hollerin' and a-goin' on about how I been shortcounting the crabs all spring, and how you and the damned Watermen's Association was gonna kick my ass from here to East Jay-zus and report me to the—"

"I never did!" my father exclaimed., "And I got a houseload of people who will testify to it! I been settin' here all afternoon mindin' my own bidness till you call me up on the phone and threaten me with—"

"Father!" The voice, deep and actressy, rang out from the crowd, and Jennifer stepped dramatically into the yard. I noticed that she positioned herself so the sunlight, filtering through the maple tree, flattered her face.

"What in the world are you doing?" she demanded in trilling accents. "What's going on here?" She looked around at my family, then at the neighbors in the shadows. "Have you people all lost your minds? Why can't we all just get along, no matter what race, color, or creed we are? Haven't we fought enough? Is that what we want our children to see? Is this how we resolve our differences?"

"Say, ain't you Carla Devane?" Ellery Swayne asked. "Look, Mertis, it's that there girl from the stories!"

"Oh, my law, it's Carla Devane, right here on the island! Kin I get your autograph?" Mertis was near to fainting.

"Is that that soap-opera girl?" someone else asked.

"We ain't had no one that famous around here since Jesus in the Islands came to the tent revival," an awed Bunky Teabury exclaimed.

56

In a flash the neighborhood mob turned from murderous to awed.

In the distance I could hear the sound of police sirens.

But the ugly mood of the moment had switched gears. People who had just been on the verge of stringing Busbee up by his own bolo tie were now clamoring to talk to his famous daughter. Folks who swore they wouldn't be caught dead watching soap operas seemed to have a suspiciously clear idea of what was what on *Hapless Hearts*. Fans were reaching out to touch Carla, clamoring for her autograph, begging her to wait right there while they went and got the camera and called Aunt Bea. In the thrill of the moment Dad and Busbee's feud was forgotten. I hustled the kids up on the relative safety of the porch and out of the various lines of fire.

"Isn't that the same speech Carla gave when the Moldavian soldiers were about to shoot Parker?" Robbie asked Callie suspiciously.

"I don't know, but I have to get her autograph!" Callie replied, deserting her post to join the press around Jennifer Clinton, who was handling her public with practiced élan.

"Thank you so much, no, no, the producers and the writers really deserve the credit! Thank you! Yes, Stud is a villain, isn't he? He's played by an actor named Robert Smith, who does a terrific job. Well, if I told you what was going to happen, then you wouldn't watch anymore. Besides, I don't really know, the writers and the producers . . ."

"Is she somebody famous?" my niece asked me.

I shrugged. "What is fame in our era of celebrity worship?" I began to ask oratorically, then decided to shut up, since I sounded pompous, even to myself.

"I don't care if Busbee is her father," Dad said to

Mom, "he's still a common, sorry bastard who ought to be killed for what he's done to the people on this island!"

A lot of people heard him say it too.

CHAPTER 6

STORY/NO STORY

MONDAY MORNING ON DEADLINE ALWAYS TASTES LIKE cold coffee in a styrofoam cup. I was musing upon this as I sat at my computer in the *Gazette* newsroom. I'd downloaded all the weekend crime and accident reports and now sat there contemplating the sheer awfulness of it all. What was my lead story?

Now, you may be asking yourself, me being right there and what with the deputies coming on the scene and all, why I didn't write up Busbee Clinton's Sunday afternoon near-lynching.

The answer is simple: I have to live here too. I may not live on Beddoe's Island anymore, but I still have to go down there. Can you imagine what hell my life would have been if I had reported a fracas that involved my family, my neighbors (most of whom are also related to me), and my childhood friend, a beloved soap diva?

I would have been the one who was lynched.

Story/no story. Besides, stuff like that happens on Beddoe's Island all the time.

I scanned the faxes, looking for someone else's troubles.

Queen Victoria Tynan, 48, and Queen Elizabeth McQueen, 52, had been arrested and charged with drunk and disorderly when they pursued their nephew, Wimber R. Stewart, 23, through the streets of Marsh Ferry with fishing rods, threatening to beat him up if they caught him. Assault with a #10 Bucktail. Could have been ugly.

Alonzo Deaver, 37, had been charged with breaking and entering and attempted robbery when he was found firmly wedged in the roof of View 'n' Chew Sub and Video Rentals at 3:00 A.M. on Sunday morning. It seemed that Deaver had attempted to break into the business by entering the kitchen through the tiny vent opening in the roof and gotten himself stuck. The neighbors, hearing his plaintive cries for help, had called 911.

Woolbert Bradley, 48, had been charged in connection with a bank robbery. Woolbert had held up the Farmers' and Watermen's Bank in Bethel last week, then returned this week to deposit his ill-gotten and marked gains in his own account. He used the same teller both times.

Over at the Firetower Mobile Home Park, Foster Turbot, 26, had been charged with second-degree murder in the death of his ace good bud Dontay Willson, 25. Seemed Foster and Dontay had drunk about three cases of beer, smoked a twenty of rock, then decided to play Russian roulette with a semiautomatic pistol.

Thus making one's chances of losing about one hundred percent. Talk about stacking the odds.

I was pondering Thoreau's comment about intelligence being finite and stupidity infinite when the phone on my desk buzzed.

"Hollis, can you come into the office?" The voice of Rig Riggle, the editor from hell, crackled over the intercom.

"We're on deadline here in the newsroom, Rig," I reminded him. Since he avoids the daily activities of the paper he allegedly edits, this small but important fact might never penetrate his gerbil-size brain.

Kevin, the county reporter, who sits next to me, stuck two pencils up his nose and crossed his eyes. It was a remarkably good imitation of either an Inuit ceremonial mask or Rig Riggle. I swatted Kevin with my Santimoke County Law Enforcement Weekend Media Information fax and tried to keep a straight face.

"Deadline?" Rig's voice asked blankly. I had a mental vision of his brain slowly scanning its information-retrieval systems for the meaning of this, the most basic and terrifying word in any newsroom. Evidently, it was alien to our alleged editor.

"Well," Rig said, not so certain now, "when you get off deadline, come to my office. That is all."

"Roger wilco, over and out," I replied sarcastically. We have a saying around here about Rig. When he was an intern he couldn't intern. When he was a reporter he couldn't report. Now that he's an editor he can't edit. Rig's sole talent seems to be his ability to suck up to the Owner. By squeezing every cent he can out of his chain of small-town rags, the Owner finances his lavish lifestyle in the south of France.

Rig's legendary incompetence is matched only by his monumental cluelessness. Example: To save the Owner a few bucks for his new yacht, Rig discontinued our subscription to the Associated Press wire. Last election we had no photo of the President to run. We have AP back now, but you never know when the next cut is coming.

After I'd translated all the accidents, DWIs, fights,

robberies, domestic incidents, and other assorted bloodlettings out of cop-ese and into neat capsule-size briefs, then sent them to the copy desk, I fooled around with a computer game for a while and read all the new Delbert cartoons on the layout table. Then I ate a couple of mints—because I wanted a cigarette—finished my cold coffee, and watched the hand on the newsroom clock crawl toward eleven. When it dropped down to a few minutes past the hour, I reluctantly shifted myself off toward Rig's office. *Abandon hope, all ye who enter here,* someone had scrawled above the door. I'll tell you, newspaper people are hilarious.

Jolene oozed out of his office in a cloud of mascara and White Diamonds. Her elaborate curls bobbed and wove as she clutched her camera and her notebook to her abundant and surgically enhanced bosoms. "I met her! I met her!" she exclaimed breathlessly, no doubt in the same orgasmic tones she uses during her Thursday afternoon trysts with Rig at the Lock and Load Motor Inn out on Route 50. Their relationship is one of the worst-kept secrets in Watertown; only Mrs. Riggle doesn't have a clue. "I got her autograph, and Riggie took my pitcher with her! She looks just like she does in the *People* magazine!"

Uh-oh.

I went in and promptly abandoned all hope.

There she was, sitting by Rig's desk, looking like a *Vanity Fair* ad in her Versace suit, long legs crossed, her eyes huge and liquid, gazing at him as if he were her last hope of salvation.

"Oh, Mr. Riggle, I can't thank you enough!" Jennifer Clinton said in her most theatrical voice.

"Oh, that's all right," Rig was drooling into his beard as he clutched her hand in his own. "The *Gazette* is

61

always happy to assist a celebrity like you, Ms. Devane."

I gulped. Riggle was guilty of a lot of things, but watching daytime drama? All this time when we thought he was locked in his office sleeping from one to two, had he actually been watching *Hapless Hearts* on the TV he claimed was always tuned to CNN? I was beginning to feel as if I was in *Invasion of the Story Snatchers.*

I was discovering that people who would swear to you that they never watched daytime TV were actually hunkered over the set with the shades drawn, addicted to daytime drama.

"Clinton. My last name is Clinton," Jen explained patiently. Seeing me, she threw her facial expression into high gear and in the same movement withdrew her hand from Rig's grasp. "Oh, Hollis!" she exclaimed, all innocence. "Your editor has agreed to let you help me research my mother's death! Isn't that wonderful?" Her breathlessness was astonishing.

Rig's shifty gaze shifted away from mine. "I want you to drop everything and get on the Renata Ringwood Clinton case," he said.

Jen Clinton batted her eyelashes at me. "I just know you can help me, being an award-winning reporter!" She gave me a wide, white smile, as if we had hatched this together and the script was playing as planned.

"Rig, if I drop everything you're going to have to cover Fosdyke et al. v. Van Nostrum in circuit. You know that if Fosdyke wins it could affect every county zoning issue for the next twenty years."

Rig, of course, was murky on the concept. But with an attractive celebrity actress sitting there gazing at him as if the sun and the moon rose and set on his face, I knew he wouldn't back down. He'd want to demonstrate that this was his world and we, the lowly reporters, were just living in it. I watched the mole in the center of his forehead turn red, as it does when he's doing what passes for thinking. Rumor has it the mole is where they put the feeder tubes when he discorporates and returns to Mars at night.

"I'll work it out," he said. "But I want you to work with Ms. . . . uh, Clinton, and use all of your contacts to look into her mother's . . . uh, death. Start now and take as long as . . . uh, you need."

"But, Rig—" I started to point out then figured what the hell. When Jen discovered there was story/no story, I'd be back in court on Fosdyke v. Van Nostrum, and Rig would look like a fool. It was an opportunity I couldn't pass up. "Sure, whatever you want," I concluded with a big fat smile.

Anyone else would have sensed my ulterior motive, but Rig didn't get where he is today with an IQ below room temperature.

"Isn't this great?" Jen beamed, regally offering him her hand. "Oh, Mr. Riggle, I can't thank you enough!"

Rig took her fingers in his and gave her his most moony stare. "Just tell me this," he sighed. "Will Carla and Prince Oleg ever get back together?"

Jennifer's laugh was like breaking crystal; I sensed that she was very aware of the power beauty gave her. "Only the writers know that, Mr. Riggle. Only the writers and God."

"Uh, uh, uh . . ."

"So," Jennifer said, turning brightly to me. "Where do we begin?"

"Lunch," I told her. "You're buying."

63

The interesting thing about my cousin Toby Russell's establishment is that no matter what it's like outside, once you walk into Toby's Bar and Grill it's always 4:00 A.M. in some dark night of the soul. The dank, smoky air is penetrated only by the light of neon beer signs, and the clack of breaking balls on the pool table competes with the R&B and country rock that Toby keeps on the jukebox. Stuffed waterfowl and fake wood paneling are the only decorator accents. The sign over the bar says WE DO NOT SERVE UNPLEASANT PEOPLE, and you'd better believe Toby means it. Of course, when you're six-six, weigh two-sixty—most of it muscle—and have entertained offers from professional wrestling, a lot of unpleasant people think it's their duty to mess with you. No one to my knowledge has tried to mess with Toby twice, but he keeps a sawed-off shotgun and a baseball bat under the bar just in case.

With the coming of warm weather, Toby had put his hair into a ponytail and trimmed his beard, revealing rugged features and the scar on his cheek. A lot of bad stuff that he doesn't talk about happened to Toby in Vietnam. He is, however, a genius in the kitchen and has won the hearts of a number of women with his haiku poetry and chocolate desserts. Toby's also my best friend. Since we're both family black sheep we have to stick together.

And, best of all, he can see and talk to Sam.

Down at Toby's Bar and Grill, he'll serve the living and the dead, but not unpleasant people of either breed.

It's funny how ghosts show up at Toby's from time to time. I guess they like his cooking and his attitude toward the living-impaired, which is: Can you pay your tab?

Happily, the bar was almost deserted at this time of

day, or I would have had to watch as ardent *Hapless Hearts* fans swarmed over Local Girl Made Good.

I was somewhat mollified by a heaping serving of spinach, mushroom, and roast chicken salad topped with Toby's secret house dressing.

But I still didn't like the idea that this snippy little actress had pulled a fast one on me. I despise being out-manipulated; it makes me feel as if I'm losing my own diabolically clever skills.

"Okay, Jen, you've won this round," I was saying. "But I promise you, when we start looking into your mother's death, you're going to find out it was an accident."

Jennifer, taking an enormous bite from her Tobyburger, beamed at the proprietor. "Oooh, this is delicious!" she cooed, dabbing ketchup from her lips. "What is your secret, Toby?"

My cousin, I noticed sourly, was as pervious as my editor to the appeal of Jen's looks. Toby was almost purring beneath Jen's eye-fluttering attention. I would have gagged, except I was too fascinated by the effect she had on men to get nauseated.

"I can't believe you didn't pay more attention to that Cadillac!" he scolded me. "After all, you were there!"

"So I saw the whole retrieval. It was an accident. Believe me, the cops looked into it."

"My mother was murdered," Jen said stubbornly, thrusting out her lower lip.

"What about Orm? What does he know?" Toby persisted.

"Friendly's the one who told me it was a story/no story," I sighed.

"But it was thirty years ago," Jennifer pointed out. "How would they know?"

"They reconstructed the scene. It was a dark, icy night; there'd been a winter storm the night before, and the roads were sheets of ice. Bridge freezes before road surface. Your mother came flying up to the bridge—probably going too fast—hit the ice on the bridge, and skidded right across the pavement, over the side, and into the water. No one even saw it; it must have been late at night. It was an accident. End of story."

Jennifer frowned. "How can you be so sure?" she demanded.

"How can *you* be so sure? And if you think your mother was murdered, who do you think did it and why? And how?"

It did me no good to watch this bone-thin woman inhaling cottage fries, nor to see her turn those enormous eyes on me in appeal. "I don't know. I just know. Please, Holly, you've got to help me! I need to find out what happened, who I am, and where I came from. You know, I was so little when she disappeared. It seems as if my life started when I went to live with my grandparents in Rochester."

"We were pretty young when you left. How come when your mother disappeared you stayed on with your grandparents up North instead of living with your father?"

Jen shrugged and frowned. She popped another fry into her mouth. "That's what I intend to find out," she said. I want to know what happened to Mother."

"What does Busbee say?"

"Not much. He never used to come see me when I was small. He'd never come up to Rochester, never had me down here." Jen paused. "But there's another reason why I came back. Your mother said you're the best reporter around."

"One of the best." Toby spoke for me.

"Well . . ." I murmured modestly.

"Then I know you can help me find out what happened. There were always so many questions, and now that she's been found there are even more." She poked a cottage fry across the plate with a long red nail. "For years and years and years I made up stories about where she was. That she was a spy, that she'd been called up on a secret mission, that she'd come back for me. And then I finally decided she'd just walked away from me. From her life. It was amazing. People would say that they'd seen her in California, in Las Vegas, in Europe. . . . My grandparents both died wondering what had happened to her. Praying she hadn't been kidnapped and raped and killed. You don't know what it's like not to know."

In an odd way I did know what she was talking about. I remembered the day, years ago, when Sam had left me standing on the dock in Fort Lauderdale as he sailed out of our week-old marriage and my life.

It was close to what she had experienced. All those years of wondering, not knowing, had created some permanent scars. I realized that they had taken their toll on Jen too.

"What brought Renata back here?" I sighed, flipping open my notebook. When I start taking notes I know I'm in.

Jennifer daintily poked a fry through a pool of ketchup. "We'd just moved up to Rochester, to Mommy and Poppy. She'd come back down to pick up some things and settle some business with Father." Suddenly, Jen looked up. "It doesn't make any sense!" she exclaimed.

"What?"

"That she would slide on the ice and go off the bridge into the water. In Rochester you drive on ice and snow all the time. Mother must have been an experienced bad-weather driver. I certainly was when I was growing up up there. She knew how to drive in bad weather. Mother grew up in upstate New York."

I bit my lip, considering what she was saying.

"Even so, accidents happen," Toby pointed out. He placed his elbows on the bar and leaned on his thickly muscled arms, stroking his chin thoughtfully. "Thirty years ago there weren't any rails on the Calais Bridge; it was just a wood plank bridge across the river. It would have been real easy to hit the icy surface and hydroplane right off there into the—"

He broke off, and the three of us contemplated being trapped in a car underwater. The pitch-black darkness, the struggle to get out of the sinking vehicle, the inexorable water seeping, then rushing, into the passenger compartment, the frantic struggle to find air to breathe, the final, certain knowledge that this was one thing you weren't going to get out of alive . . . that you were going to die in the dark water.

I shuddered. I hate closed spaces. Toby shook his head.

Jennifer swallowed. "Dear God," she said succinctly.

I cleared my throat. "How do you think that someone would get your mother to go off the bridge?"

"I don't know," Jen said edgily. She looked down at her empty plate, where a smear of ketchup pooled like blood. "But they could do it, couldn't they?"

"Sure. You can put a dead body in a car and send it off a bridge; that part's pretty easy. You just shove the body into the front seat and use something like a stone or a brick to hold down the accelerator pedal." I have to wonder what Toby did in 'Nam when he comes out with casual remarks like that, but I know I'll never find out.

"Motive," I said. "The state may not need a motive to go after a murder, but this reporter does. Who would want to kill Renata? And why?"

Jen frowned. "I don't know. I was just a little kid. We'd just moved back to Rochester, to Genesee Street with Mommy and Poppy, and Mom said she had to make one more trip back." She closed her eyes. "She told me that when she came back we'd be rich, and we wouldn't have to live with Mommy and Poppy, that we could go anywhere we wanted, anywhere in the world. She wanted to go somewhere warm, somewhere where there were tropical beaches."

"Do you think Busbee did her in?" I asked bluntly.

Jen shrugged. "I don't know. I've been trying not to think that my own father would—" She shook her head. "But you do think about it, you know. You can't help but wonder. It doesn't make staying with him any easier. In fact, I'm thinking of moving into one of the bed-and-breakfast places on the island while I'm here. He's not the easiest man in the world to get along with. Besides, he seems to hate company. I could almost think he is ashamed of me. The other night this man came by, and I would have sworn he did everything but *order* me to stay in my room. . . ."

But I wasn't really listening. I was thinking. "Is cousin Larry LaMonte still having the county impound yard at his gas station?" I asked Toby. "I haven't noticed lately."

"When last heard from. He's been runnin' that county yard since I was a boy. Doubt they'd give it to anyone else. You can pick your nose, and you can pick your fruit, but you can't pick your family," he added sourly.

I winced. Thinking about Larry makes me do that. "Jen, did you sign anything to dispose of your mother's car?" I grabbed her arm. "I mean, you are her sole heir, right?"

"Yes, I am her heir. Mommy and Poppy are dead. I have some papers and stuff, but I haven't signed anything yet. I wanted to come down here first—"

"Okay. We've got the same chance a snowball has in hell, but *if* the Caddy's *still* in Larry's junkyard, and *if* we can find it, and *if* we *don't* find something in the passenger compartment, will you believe that your mother's death was an accident?"

Jen's eyes opened wide, and she smiled the first real smile I'd seen from her since she was five years old. "Yes," she agreed.

This, I thought, should be easy. I'd be back in court and listening to Fosdyke under cross-examination before the day was out.

Larry Lamonte, my mother's aunt's son's nephew, was at his usual stand, a ruined aluminum kitchen chair beside the shack he calls both home and office at LaMonte's Auto Salvage and Recycling on Red Toad Road. While a tattered Confederate flag whipped proudly in the breeze above his head, he spat his chew into a coffee can at his feet and perused the latest issue of *Soldier of Fortune.* Somewhere in the depths of the tin and tarpaper dwelling he calls home, Rush Limbaugh blared, ignored.

Walter, his ancient and senile pit bull, slept on his back on the crumbling asphalt, opening one eye and growling at us in a half-threatening way as he rose unsteadily to his feet and came over to express his affection by sniffing my crotch. When you have a twelve- or fourteen-year-old car

70

with more than 200,000 miles on it, you get to do lots of business with Larry and Walter.

"Well, now!" Larry cackled over his magazine. "Son of a bitch if it ain't Cousin Holly! Whatever it is you want, I don't know nothin' about it, 'specially them stolen C.V. boots! I already tole the goddamned pigs that! I don't know nothin' about norh—" When he got a good look at Jen he halted in midspeech. "Hel-lo, little lady!"

While Walter said hello to my leg I made the introductions.

"I watch *The Young and the Restless*," he said, rather shamefaced, after I told him Jennifer was a soap diva, but he rewarded us with a glimpse of his rotting yellow teeth as he looked at her with appreciation. "Anyway, if you really are Carla Devane, how come you ain't in New Yawk on the air?" It was a question, I blush to admit, that should have occurred to me and hadn't. I was quite interested in my childhood friend's reply.

Jennifer gave him a dazzling smile. "I've been written out for a while. There were some things happening. . . . Carla's recuperating from her amnesia ordeal in a chic clinic in Paris. You can help me, can't you, Larry?"

Once again I was fascinated to see how far you could get on beauty and celebrity.

Larry was not only storing the Coupe de Ville until the police released it to Jen, but he generously allowed as how Jen could keep it there as long as she wanted. "Them pigs don't like me to allow anyone to poke through the impound lot, but seeing as how you're on the stories and it was your mom's car, I guess we can make an exception. A man still got some rights on his own goddamned property, even in this po-lice state!"

Since he collected a generous rent from the state in

exchange for allowing them to store their impounded autos on his fenced lot, his militia-inspired attitude toward law enforcement seemed a bit churlish, but who am I to argue with a purveyor who gives a family discount on chopped parts? All that counted to me was that Cousin Larry had the key that opened the chain-link gates and he was willing to allow us in.

We found the Coupe de Ville at the back of the auto graveyard between a Lexus with bullet holes in the windshield and a burned-out Chevy Sierra pickup that still smelled of marijuana smoke. It sat on its flattened tires, drying out in the April sunlight, still reeking of river mud and mildew. Both the hood and the trunk were wide open, sporting the dents made by the crowbars of the investigators.

Evidently, it had not wintered over well.

"Wow!" Jennifer said when she got a full whiff of the Caddy. She took a step back and so did I. It smelled like a hundred thousand dead crabs that had been baking in the summer sun for a month. And it didn't look much better. The faded red paint was peeling away from the metal, oysters and barnacles had spatted on the fenders, and the windshield was smashed into spiderwebs of cracks. Through the open windows we could see thick white strings of mold growing happily on the former leather and plush interior.

The mold looked like Santa Claus's beard—if Santa were played by Vincent Price. The doors, long ago rusted shut, no longer opened in spite of our best efforts. The recovery team had smashed the driver-and passenger-side windows to run the pull chain through the compartment; sharded glass glittered in the sunlight.

"Ugh," I mumbled. "I'm not real sure we should . . . that stuff could make you sick . . . spores . . ."

"One time when I was struggling, I had to fall into a pit full of snakes for a B movie," Jennifer said, taking off her jacket and handing it to me. "After that you can face almost anything." She looked me over critically. "I'm a lot smaller than you are, so it will be easier for me to crawl in."

She dove into the passenger compartment through the open window, and the long, hairy strings of white mold parted, then closed around her. I watched as her pantyhose ran and her stiletto-heeled pumps waved wildly in the air, and I began to revise my feelings about her helplessness as she disappeared into the rank, moist interior.

"God, you wouldn't believe how it stinks in here." Her voice echoed hollowly from the floor space, and she started coughing. The car rocked back and forth.

"Get out of there," I begged her. "Please."

"No way," Jen's muffled voice drifted upward. "Jeez, the keys are still in the ignition! Ouch! I cut myself on a crab shell! This reminds me of the time Carla's plane crashed over Egypt and she was eluding Sheik Abdul's men because he wanted to add her to his harem, and she fell into this forgotten pharaoh's tomb and was rescued by Dr. Whip Remington, the famous archaeologist and spy for the C.I.A. and—ah!"

As I watched she emerged from the mold, blinking in the light.

She held out a brick—not just any brick, but a brick with a piece of rusting baling wire artfully wrapped around it like a Christmas present.

Jen pushed a finger between the flat of the brick and the wire to show the space. Her expression, as she handed it to me, was grim.

"Just right for weighting down the accelerator pedal, don't you think?"

CHAPTER 7

THE WEIGHT OF EVIDENCE

I'LL GIVE JEN CREDIT FOR THIS: THE GIRL KNEW HOW to pick her battles. She also kept a spare pair of pantyhose in her pocketbook, and was limber enough to change in the passenger seat of a Honda. "I learned how to do this going from audition to audition when I was starting out," she told me.

"I'm speechless with admiration," I replied, watching her contortions. And I was.

The state police barracks on Route 50 is the lair from which Friendly operates.

"I hope your friend can help us," Jen said as we walked past a group of uniformed policepeople clustering beside the building, sucking down their forbidden cigarettes. Both Jen and I lifted our noses to inhale the smell of burning tobacco.

"Take an Altoid," she cautioned.

Friendly's tiny office was as cluttered as his personal life. Battered file cabinets hung open, and posters advertising procedures for safe handling of human-body products and handgun safety hung on the walls. Ormand Friendly himself, resplendent in a hideous blue and purple madras jacket and a tie featuring the Grateful Dead dancing bears, was hunched over his desk with a phone to each ear, surrounded by several deep stacks of law-enforcement paperwork. A half-eaten cheese steak with fried onions, wrapped in greasy paper, spread across the top of one stack. "Uh-hunh, uh-hunh, uh-hunh, uh-hunh," he was saying as Jen and I wandered into his dingy office.

Friendly winked carelessly at me as he stuffed a triplicate form into the ancient Royal and began some seriously slow two-fingered typing. "Uh-hunh, uh-hunh, uh-huh, uh-huuh," he mumbled, hunting and pecking away. "Oh. Okay. Uh-huh."

Then he saw Jennifer.

Friendly's green eyes roamed up and down her Versace suit, and she gave him her most dazzling smile.

"I'll call you back," my cop pal said abruptly, cradling the phone. Forms were forgotten as he swiveled around in his chair, giving Jen a sappy grin. If this had been a cheap fifties movie you would have heard the brassy jazz in the background. Friendly actually shambled to his feet. "Can I help you?" he asked her.

Jennifer gave a little frisson as she held out her hand to him. "Oh, you must be Detective Sergeant Friendly," she said. "I'm Jennifer Clinton. Hollis has told me so much about you."

Actually, I'd given her the short version, but I had to admire the way she worked a room. Jen may have been raised in upstate New York, but she had all the killer instincts of a southern belle. She had turned on the actress thing full blast. "Holly says you're the man I need to talk to, Sergeant," she purred.

What can I say? Friendly's a guy. His testosterone went into overdrive. He ate up her fluttering as if she were one of Toby's soft crab sandwiches and came back for more. The mountain of paperwork was laid aside, and his gaze was fixed solidly on Jen.

"We've been waiting for you to sign some papers so we can release your mother's remains and her possessions," he said as he dove into one of his file cabinets and came up with yet more paper. I have yet to

75

see a cop shop where no one is drowning in paperwork. You even have to fill out forms to get more forms.

Jennifer merely glanced at the documents he provided for her. Then she sighed. "Sergeant Friendly, I need help."

She placed the brick squarely on the desk between them. Some rust crumbled off the wire, flaking across his papers.

Friendly glanced at it, then sat back down in his wobbly office chair, listening attentively to Jen's suspicions about the causes of her late mother's death.

One so very rarely runs into well-groomed, articulate, attractive people in the criminal-justice system that I really felt no resentment, only a vague surprise that he didn't seem to recognize Jennifer as soap diva Carla Devane. Could it be that Ormand Friendly was the only human being in a five-county area who didn't watch *Hapless Hearts?*

Sometimes, I thought, watching her striking poses, she herself probably doesn't know the difference between Jennifer Clinton and Carla Devane. Out of the corner of my eye I noticed that an awful lot of people seemed to have an excuse to linger around Friendly's open door. The cop grapevine must have been on overdrive. But, hey, when the most exciting people you run into are under arrest, a genuine celebrity, however minor, was big news in this neck of the woods.

When Jen finished, Friendly nodded and leaned forward in his chair, poking the brick with a pencil. "We've got a pretty thorough forensics team, Ms. Clinton. If there were something as suspicious as this in your mother's car, they would have noticed it." He shrugged. Jennifer made a small, almost inaudible hissing sound. I had the feeling she was not used to being denied.

I knew Friendly caught lots of harassment from hysterical survivors of the accidented, suicided, and even the naturally deceased. They often feel a need to believe that their loved one was the victim of foul play from nameless enemies or imaginary serial killers; denial is a way of coping with senseless tragedy. Friendly smoothly launched into his usual reassuring patter. "It was thirty years ago, Ms. Clinton," he concluded gently.

But Jennifer was made of harder material than most. "I'm sure the forensics team carefully picked out all the human remains, which would be mostly bone, but perhaps repelled by the smell and the slime they wouldn't have looked for anything else at the bottom of the passenger compartment." She abruptly shifted into imperious mode. "I'd like you to speak to those people again and ask them what else they might have missed when they recovered my mother's body after thirty years down there under the water."

"Well, I . . . I . . ." he sputtered. I'd never seen Friendly flapped before, and it was fun to watch. He squinted at the brick and poked at the rusting wire again, a little less certainly. But he wouldn't commit. Hey, I could have told her he was commitment phobic.

"I think it's quite easy to see that this could have been used to weigh down the accelerator pedal, and that my mother, dead or alive, could have been placed behind the wheel and sent off the bridge," Jen continued, tapping her nails impatiently on the desk.

Friendly sighed and shook his head. "That might make a good script for one of your soap operas, but the chances of its happening in real life are pretty slender." He rose from his chair, pushing his hands deep into his pockets, a signal that we were dismissed. "But just to put your mind at ease I'll double-check with the divers and the forensics team, all right?" He shuffled some papers on his desk.

Jennifer nodded. "You do that." But she gave him her dazzling smile again as she picked up her brick. "I'll be waiting to hear from you. And you'll also have all the material in my mother's file photocopied for me?"

Friendly merely nodded. He ran a finger around his shirt collar, as if his Grateful Dead tie were strangling him.

As Jen stepped out into the hall she was swamped with uniformed fans who bore her gently away to meet the barracks commander.

"What the pluperfect hell is this all about, hon?" Friendly asked me irritably.

I closed my eyes. "Rig Riggle," I sighed, and sketched in the rest of the story for him.

"Want me to kill him for you?" Friendly suggested cheerfully. I *think* he was joking. But Rig has that shrieking chalk-on-a-blackboard effect on people, so you never know. Rig's had death threats from the nuns over at St. Morpheme's.

"No," I decided after some consideration. "With my luck we'd get caught." I frowned. "Besides, as nutty as this all seems, I'm not entirely certain there isn't something here. Whether or not Renata was a homicide, this is becoming much more interesting than Fosdyke v. Van Nostrum."

"What's that?" Friendly asked. "Civil case?"

"Oh, two Three Rs—you know, rich, retired, Republican—are lawyering each other. Seems Fosdyke says Van Nostrum's new deck blocks the morning sunlight in a corner of his bedroom."

Friendly chuckled. "Wait'll Judge Carroll hears that one. He doesn't suffer fools and frivolous lawsuits gladly."

"That's why I wanted to cover it. It would be so much fun. Frank would be at his most sarcastic." I looked at my watch. "I guess it will have to go unreported on for now."

"A lost Pulitzer indeed," Friendly said gravely. "Good Lord, where do you find your friends, Hollis? This actress is gonna cause me some trouble now. You know she's gonna get the lieutenant on her side next, then I'm gonna get dragged in." He pushed a hand through his hair, looking more than ever like Harrison Ford ridden hard and put away wet. "God, I hate cold cases. The thing is, after a lot of running around and to'ing and fro'ing and unnecessary bullshit, it's comin' down to the same thing, hon. Mama took a header on an icy bridge and went over the side. Jesus, haven't I got enough to worry about with all the damned rock stars shootin' each other?"

But I wasn't thinking about our local drug wars. I wanted to agree with Friendly, that Renata Ringwood Clinton's death was a tragic accident, but something about that brick nagged at me, although I would have been hard-pressed to explain it to rational Ormand Friendly. God, I could barely explain why I wasn't plunging into a full-fledged, kick-out-the-jams paper-back-novel romance with the man, except to say been there, done that, and have the scars to prove it as far as men were concerned.

But it wasn't romance that was lighting up my pal's life at the moment. "Don't forget, hon," he said happily. "Fishing Friday night. We're meeting Toby at the harbor at five. I'm bringing the beer. You bring the bait, and Tobe will have the food. They're catching rock off Cook's Point," Friendly continued in wistful tones. "I'm livin' through this week for that first strike, that first cold beer, that first whiff of Bay breeze, lemme tell ya. This could be the best rock season in years. One of the baby troopers caught a big ole ten-pounder off the Swann's Island light last night. I can't wait to get a rod in my hands!"

I felt the same way. "I'll be there or be square. An evening of going after the big rock will be heaven after a week like this," I promised. My dating life consisted of some high romance, as you can see. But fishing with Friendly was about all the passion I felt equipped to handle right now. In the love wars I was a shell-shocked veteran who wasn't dying to get back in the battle.

"I don't think your friend is exactly leaping to solve this," Jennifer sighed as we climbed back into my car.

"What did you expect? It's a cold case. Look, Jen, you don't have any proof, except for a brick that someone could have tossed into the car at any time since it came out of the river. You don't even know who would kill your mother or why."

"Yeah, but I'll bet my father does," Jen replied.

CHAPTER 8

OLD HUSBANDS' TALES

CONFRONTING BUSBEE IN HIS DEN WAS NOT AT THE TOP of my list of fun things to do. Nonetheless, I found myself driving back down the road to Beddoe's Island again, a nervous Jennifer in tow.

"He's got to tell me what he knows," she said several times, which made her rather dull company.

The old Clinton homeplace was a rambling Victorian, set off by itself at the Bay end of the island at Turkey Buzzard Point. If it hadn't been surrounded by trash, tumbledown crab floats, and the concrete bunker that had once served as the Clinton's Seafood packing house, it might have been even less attractive. It was built in the glory days of the Bay steamer, when the island was riding an economic high on the oyster trade. A century later, the turreted and bay-windowed edifice had begun to look more and more like the old Addams homeplace with each passing year.

When I was a kid and used to ride my bike out here to see Jen, it had been on the verge of neglect. Now it had slipped over the edge into a forlorn wreck.

The white paint was all but peeled away, and the tattered gingerbread fretwork dangled froth the pillars of the wraparound porches. The foundation was caving in from rot and pesthole beetles. A couple of windows in the third-floor turret were broken out and had been replaced with plywood. The slate roof looked as if it were sliding off the pitch. An aura of decay, as palpable as the aroma of last summer's crab shells, shrouded the property.

Busbee's decision to add the packing houses and sheds to the landscape hadn't helped matters; they, in their turn, had deteriorated over the years until the whole place looked like a combat zone of decomposing crab sheds, ancient wire pots, battered concrete bunkers, and the sad detritus of the vanishing seafood industry. As the Bay died, so did the crabs and the fish and the oysters.

Only Busbee's brand-new purple Cadillac, all

glittering chrome and fresh paint, stood out from the gently eroding landscape. William Faulkner would have felt right at home.

"Grim, isn't it?" Jennifer asked, but she expected no answer as she swung out of my car and, clutching her brick, marched up the creaking steps into the house.

I followed her uncertainly, certain that no good and a lot of ugliness was going to happen soon.

Inside, the house was still and dusty, neglect hanging in the air along with the dust motes. Not much seemed to have changed since I was a kid, except everything had gotten older and dustier. The place smelled of age—that faint, not unpleasant odor of dry rot and ancient leather-bound books.

As I followed Jen through the front hall I glanced into the parlor, where horsehair furniture that must have belonged to Busbee's great-grandparents reposed beneath holland sheets and a thick coat of dust. Hundred-year-old damask curtains hung in fragile tatters.

When we were kids we used to play in there on rainy days. There was a big old curio cabinet looming in the corner, where previous generations had stashed their bric-a-brac and treasures, fantastical and wonderful stuff like blown-glass animals and Chelsea bow shepherdesses and mourning lockets made from the braided human hair of the long dead.

Renata had the key, and she would open the cabinet to let us take down the china dogs and glass-headed dolls and souvenir seashells. We were allowed to play with them if we were careful. Busbee and Renata weren't big on antiques, as I recalled. I noted that the cabinet was still there, although I sort of doubted that anyone had even opened it in thirty years. Like

82

everything else in the unused parlor, it looked cobwebbed and forlorn.

Had the place been this desolate when we were kids? I didn't remember. Kids don't pay attention to things like that. Before I could explore my memories further, Jen strode into the kitchen at the back of the house.

"Father!" she called in an exasperated tone as she marched into the room, where a stack of dirty pots was piled in the sink and a fly buzzed around the open butter dish on the sticky table. A frying pan with an inch of grease in the bottom sat on the encrusted old gas stove. Judging by the open jars and wrappers, Busbee had evidently eaten a hearty lunch of fried peanut butter and bacon sandwiches on Wonder bread.

"Faaather!" Jen called again, looking around irritably. "God, he is *such* a slob," she muttered. "And such a miser. This peanut butter isn't even a store brand! You'd think he'd at least spend the money to hire someone to clean this place. I'm not doing it!" She sounded like a woman at the end of her rope. "Faaaather! Are you home?"

From behind us there was a faint grunt and the sound of splashing water.

"He's a taking *another* bath," she said, inclining her head toward a closed door, where faint sounds of running water could be heard. "It seems as if all the man does in his spare time is soak in that tub. He says it's good for his nerves." Her tone implied that she didn't think much of the curative properties of tub bathing. She looked more like a shower person to me.

Jen rapped smartly on the bathroom door. "Father! I need to talk to you! Please come out of there!" she commanded.

"Can't a man soak in his own house?" Busbee's voice

rose querulously, along with the sound of splashing.

"Not when you're soaking in the only bathroom in the house!" Jen replied crisply. "Besides, we have company. Holly Ball is here."

There was a moment of dead silence. I could almost feel Busbee turning this one over in his mind. "I'm a poor man," he finally whined. "I ain't got nothin' to say, and I ain't making no comments to no newspapers neither. You tell her to go away." There were some more splashing sounds, then he added, "Whyn't you go back to New York 'n' leave me in peace? I'm a poor man. I barely have enough to hold body and soul together."

Jennifer closed her fist and pounded on the door. "I'm not going back to New York until you answer some of my questions, you miserable old man! I'll stay here all summer if I have to, but sooner or later you're gonna tell me what I want to know!"

"Go away! And take that there Ball gal with you!" Busbee's voice drifted through the door. I could almost imagine him in there, modestly clutching a mildewed washrag to his chest, but I stopped myself just in time. There are some things that humanity was not meant to contemplate, and a buck-naked Busbee Clinton was one of them. "Get back to New York! I ain't gonna give you anything, including my money!"

Jen turned to look at me. "He's got it into his head that I am down here after his 'fortune,' " she explained in the puzzled voice of a woman who makes enough each year to buy and sell the average working person. She leaned against the door. "Damn it, Father, you come out of there right this minute!"

With the flat of her hand Jen struck the wood hard enough to make the door shake in the frame. There were groans and mutterings and splashes from behind the door.

After a brief wait Busbee made a damp entrance, wearing the same bathrobe he'd sported the previous night when he showed up so unexpectedly at my folks' house. He looked at me without interest and immediately waddled toward the wheezing Kelvinator, leaving a trail of watery footprints across the linoleum. He scrambled around in its innards and came up with a bottle of cheap bourbon, into which he dropped two Maalox tablets.

"Father, Hollis is here to find out more about my mother," Jen said with vast carelessness for the truth.

He swigged thirstily from the bottle, then thrust it back into the refrigerator, regarding me suspiciously. "I ain't got nothin' to say to no one from the newspaper, especially if it's one o' them Balls," he said in a surly mumble. "But you can print this much and stick my name on it. I'm a poor man, just trying to make an honest living, and I spent my whole life trying to do the Christian thing, and this is the thanks I get!"

"Oh, please stop that," Jen snapped. "That *Beverly Hillbillies* act is so beat."

Busbee gave her a bleary look, then turned his attention on me. "I don't want nothin' from you in that goddamned. excuse for a newspaper. I don't even want no Balls hangin' around my house at all. If my daughter doesn't know who the enemy is, I do, and it's any kid of Perk and Doll Balls!"

I was more than happy to oblige the old poop by getting the hell out of that house of health-department horrors, but Jen wasn't having any of it.

"I want to know what happened to my mother!" she shouted. "She was murdered! And you know something, I know you do!"

85

Busbee belched into his closed fist. His bloodshot eyes shifted uneasily around the room, and he fingered the gold chains around his neck. "You show some respect for your father!" he grunted. "You're accusin' me of murder!"

Jen drew herself up to her full height, Carla Devane to the core. I wondered again if she knew the difference between real life and daytime drama.

"I . . . want . . . to . . . know . . . what happened . . . to . . . my . . . mother," she said through her teeth. With a theatrical flourish she withdrew the wired brick from her pocketbook and placed it on the table.

I guess we were both expecting Busbee to recoil in horror, like Dracula exposed to a crucifix, but he just stared at it, sitting there next to the peanut butter. The wire flaked some rust across the tabletop.

"What the hell is that?" Busbee asked. "Get it away from my peanut butter; it's messin' up the clean tabletop!"

That tabletop hadn't been clean since the Korean War, but I wasn't going to point that out. I had started backing out of the room.

Jen stood her ground. "I found this in the bottom of Mother's car," she hissed. "Someone used it to weigh down the accelerator pedal."

I was about to point out that we didn't know that for a fact, but I was distracted by a knock on the back door.

"Busbee? Are you home?" H. P. Wescott, Sam's father, peered through the screen.

We looked at each other.

I don't know who was more surprised. It was like going to the moon and seeing your next-door neighbor over the next crater. My former father-in-law, known in the family as the Old Man, is one of the richest and most powerful men not just in Santimoke County, not just on the Eastern Shore, but in the entire state of Maryland, maybe the Mid-Atlantic region. The Old Man's real-estate and development interests make him a nine-hundred-pound gorilla, as in where does a nine-hundred-pound gorilla sit? Anywhere he pleases. He is not my favorite person, nor am I his. And he was still not too thrilled with me since I'd uncovered that big scandal about Wescott Development Corp. (motto: "Pave the Bay") trying to fill and build on some protected wetlands, especially since he'd tried to bribe me into ignoring the whole thing.

Wescotts, dead or alive, are the bane of my existence.

But wait, there was more.

"Is he in there? Is he in there? Where's the Ornamental Hermit, Busbee?" I looked past H.P. and straight into the face of the Poultry Prince himself. Billy Chinaberry was squinting through the wire mesh, trying to see over the Old Man's shoulder.

This was getting interesting.

"Jesus H. Christ in a handbasket!" Busbee cursed, drawing his ratty robe together again. He shifted from one bare foot to the other. "Can't a man have no peace in his own house? What the hell are you two doin' here?"

But it was too late. With his usual assumption that he was welcome anyplace he chose to grace with his presence, H.P. was inside the house, with Chinaberry right on his heels.
Chinaberry looked like a man who needed an obituary; his skin was the color of an old sheet, and there was a slight tremor to his chin and hands that I didn't like. But his expression was thunderous.

"What's she doing here?" they both asked at once.

I haven't spent the past decade reporting stuff people would rather I didn't without hearing that question asked. Usually it means something's being concealed. My reporter instincts twitched.

"They're just leaving," Busbee growled.

"I'm not leaving until I get some answers," Jennifer insisted.

"It looks the Billionaire Boys' Club is in session." I whipped out my notebook. "Have any comment for the press, H.P.?"

I got a look that should have intimidated. When I first met Sam, H.P. had terrified me. Not anymore. I knew him too well now, and I had too much on him.

"How about you, Mr. Chinaberry?" Since he hadn't done anything to me I had no quarrel with the Poultry Prince.

But Chinaberry seemed not to notice me at all. He was looking at Jennifer as if he were seeing a ghost. Slowly, his eyes grew wide and his mouth opened and closed, but no words came out.

H.P. left off glaring at me long enough to see what Chinaberry was looking at. "I'll be damned," he said softly.

My estimation of rich old white guys, which had never been really high, dropped a couple more points. Surely H.P. had better things to do than watch *Hapless Hearts*? Didn't being president emeritus of a chicken empire keep Billy Chinaberry busy enough to avoid daytime drama?

Busbee shrugged. "This is Renata's daughter." He admitted this with reluctance, then added, "Them two was just leaving."

"Not until I get some answers," Jennifer said again. She crossed her arms over her chest and looked mulish.

"My Lord," H.P. exclaimed. "I thought for a minute you were your mother. You look so much like her."

"You could be her twin," Billy Chinaberry said slowly. He couldn't seem to take his eyes off Jen.

"I could?" Vanity made her easy to distract, I noted. No doubt she also thought they were fans of Carla Devane. Once again, I thought, beauty and celebrity won the day for Jen.

H.P. and Chinaberry exchanged an uneasy look. It was barely a flicker, but I noticed it.

"You knew Renata Ringwood Clinton?" I asked them.

"We all knew her," Billy Chinaberry said dourly. "Where do you think—"

H.P. grunted. "So what do you want? We don't know any more than you do."

"I want to know how my mother died," Jen said. "I want some answers, and I want them now. I've waited almost thirty years to find out what happened."

Busbee had been silent, as watchful as a spider. "She wants to get her hands on my money!" he whined. "That's what she wants! That's what you all want. Well, there ain't none! So you can all go on about your business and leave me alone."

"Don't cut the fool, Busbee," H.P. said sharply. But he was studying Jennifer as if he hadn't heard her speak. "By God," he said to her, "if I didn't know better, I'd think you were Renata all over again."

"Isn't that the truth," Chinaberry said. His hands shook as he dug into the pocket of his well-tailored jacket and produced a cell phone. "Hold my meeting with the Cluck Cluck Chicken Shack people until four," he barked without a greeting. "Something's come up and I'll be delayed. Let Cushman make his presentation,

89

and I'll try to get there as soon as I can." He slapped the device shut again. "How much do they know?" he asked Busbee.

He was rewarded with a bald eyeball look. "They don't know nothing," Busbee growled. "And they don't need to know nothing. Our business don't concern them." He used the sleeve of his dingy bathrobe to wipe his forehead. In spite of the dankness, he was perspiring.

"You were here the other night, weren't you?" Jennifer asked Billy Chinaberry. "I thought I recognized your voice. But Father told me to stay upstairs, that it was a business matter."

Busbee hissed between his teeth.

H.P. reluctantly tore his gaze away from Jennifer long enough to survey me with distaste. "See here, what do you know about the Ornamental Hermit, Hollis?" he asked.

"The Ornamental wha—" I started to say, then I remembered an old reporter's trick: If you want information, pretend you know more than you really do. Sometimes you can get the other person to reveal all kinds of interesting stuff that way. "Oh, that. Don't tell me the two richest men on the Eastern Shore are interested in that?"

Billy Chinaberry licked his lips. "You're damned right we're interested in it," he said. "And Busbee has no right to keep it from us. He must have known all this time that it wasn't with Renata when she went overboard. If it was, they would have found it in the car."

I was hoping Jen would ask what the Ornamental Hermit was at that point, because the answer would have enlightened me too. Instead, she had grown weary of the attention focused on someone other than herself.

90

"Who are these men? I don't think anyone's thought to introduce us."

"You don't need to know that either," Busbee said quickly.

"He's H. P. Wescott, and I'm Billy Chinaberry," Chinaberry announced. "We're your—"

H.P. made a gesture. "You've said enough, Billy." He turned to Busbee. "We're here because you called us. You said you knew the whereabouts of the Ornamental Hermit."

There was a silence you could have sliced with a knife.

"I never called you," Busbee finally sputtered. "I'm not givin' any of the money back neither!"

"My God, man, use some common sense," H.P. snapped.

"Or at the very least exercise some taste." Billy Chinaberry gave him a disdainful look. "You called my office and told my secretary that you knew where the Ornamental Hermit is."

"That's the message I got too!" H.P. said. He looked at his watch. "You took me out of a meeting with Hiromoto Industries! I've left a bunch of puzzled Japanese executives sittin' around with a sixty-million-dollar deal on the table!"

Busbee sucked on his teeth, glowering at both of them. "I never called nobody," he sulked. "I been settin' in the tub mindin' my own bidness all morning, ever since I got back from town. You can ast anybody! I was down at the bank in Watertown all morning!"

This sounded faintly familiar to me. Hadn't he had a similar excuse when he'd denied calling Dad last night? Evidently, weirdo phone pranks were Busbee's way of getting his jollies off. He wouldn't be the first drunk, or

91

the last, to use the phone as an instrument of torture.

"Well, if you didn't call me, who did?" H.P. asked. "When Mavis told me you'd left a message about the Ornamental Hermit, I knew it was you!"

"Same here," Chinaberry said. "Look here, Busbee, H.P. and I are busy men. We don't have time to fart around with your foolishness. What do you want? More money? Because—"

"That's enough of that!" H.P. cut in. His pager beeped. "If you know where the Ornamental Hermit is, have out with it! If you don't, don't waste my time."

"It's got to be somewhere," Chinaberry fretted. "If it had been in the car—"

"Shut up, Billy," H.P. cut him off brusquely. "This is not a matter for public discussion. I've got to get back to the office, and I suggest you do the same. As to you two"—he waved his pager at Busbee and me—"I don't know what you've got cooked up here, but I'll tell you what's what. If I see a word about me in that rag of a newspaper or get any more of these prank phone calls, I'll buy the goddamned *Gazette* and the first thing I'll do is fire you!" He stepped closer to Busbee. He was much the taller of the two. "And you, Busbee, any more of your cheap tricks and I'll see you in hell!"

"I din' do nothin'," Busbee whined, taking a step back.

Chinaberry seemed unable to drag his gaze away from Jennifer. It didn't seem to me to be the sort of adoring look she was accustomed to receiving from men, though. Rather, he looked puzzled and ill.

"I—" he started to say, but H.P. dropped a heavy paw on his shoulder, pulling him toward the door.

"Let's get the hell out of here," H.P. commanded.

"But—" Chinaberry continued to stare at the actress.

"Now," H.P. said, and almost forced the poultry magnate out the door.

As the screen swung back on its hinges, I thought I heard the Old Man tell Chinaberry to let the lawyers handle it.

In their wake they left a silence.

It was only when the sound of car tires on gravel broke the stillness that Jennifer spoke.

"I want to know what happened to my mother," she said.

"What's the Ornamental Hermit?" I asked right behind her.

"That's it! Out!" Busbee choked, almost dancing with rage. He stabbed a stubby finger at Jennifer. "I want you out of here right now or I'll call the cops!"

CHAPTER 9

YOU SAY YOU WANT A REVELATION

"BED AND BREAKFAST? BED AND BREAKFAST?" MY mother was outraged. "Of course you won't stay in one of those places! They don't change the sheets! Like that place down the road that's run by hippies," she added, gesturing toward the end of the street where Grimsby House, formerly the old Grimsby place, was open for business under a fresh coat of paint and a lot of busy chintz.

Mertis Swayne, who cooked the breakfasts, said you could barely see the bloodstains on the floorboards anymore, and if you didn't already know you'd hardly believe that all those awful things had happened there back in the sixties. It's a good thing the tourists don't know that the place had such a bad reputation on the island that the V.F.D. used it for years as their Halloween Haunted Crack House.

"They're not hippies, Mom." I tried to correct her for the sake of accuracy. "They're New Agers." I was a little leery of the trend-sucking California couple myself, but facts are facts.

"Be that as it may," Doll said firmly, "I don't see why Jennifer has to stay in a house where people roll rocks all over each other and burn those oils."

"They're crystals, and those oils are aromatherapy, or something." I was a little fuzzy on the concept myself, but Mom was having none of it. I half expected her to say it was all the devil's work, but she's often more sophisticated than I give her credit for.

"Imagine allowing your childhood friend to stay with foreigners," Mom sniffed, getting right back on track. "And poor Jennifer a local born!"

"Oh, Miss Doll." Jen was grateful.

"You stay here with us, you poor thing," Mom told her as we picked our way through the latest pile of yard-sale clothes and other junk that people had donated and my mother was now sorting out for the V.F.D. Spring Fling flea market. When we arrived safely in the kitchen, the washing machine was putting a load of dingy whites through the spin cycle. Never let it be said that Doll Ball, the Rummage Sale Queen of Beddoe's Island, ever sold a gray secondhand pair of tube socks or size 44D push-up bra to the unsuspecting public. I absently picked a baby bonnet off one of my father's decoys and began folding stuff to conceal a rude sigh of relief.

"I'd ask you to stay at my house," I said politely, "but I have to work, and you'd have to sleep on my ratty fold-out couch, and the cat's peed on it, and I can't quite get the smell out." For once I was grateful for Venus, the Cat with an Attitude. All I needed was for Sam to show up unexpectedly and scare the living hell out of Jen. I like to give him warning about overnight guests.

"Oh, Miss Doll, could I stay with you? Just until I can get some information about my mother?" Jen and my mother clutched each other's hands as if this were the Friday fade-out and you'd have to wait until Monday afternoon to find out what happened next.

"You stay here as long as you like." In the living room my father looked up from his newspaper long enough to add his two cents. "I can't believe that son of a bitch Busbee Clinton put his own daughter out. No, you stay right here, honey."

Mom glared at him, not because she disagreed with what he said, but because she was getting sick of his haunting the house all day, getting underfoot. "I wish these watermen would go back to work," she said in an undertone. "This crabbers' strike is trouble all over the island."

As she spoke she produced a freshly made strawberry pie and began to cut us both generous slices. I poured coffee into thick white ironstone mugs. Home again.

I might have been five years old, so little had changed, I thought, listening to Jen give my mother her anxiety about the fate of Renata. I took a bite of pie and surrendered to the bliss of Doll's comfort food.
Mom listened to Jen as she folded a stack of OshKosh B'Gosh overalls on the Formica kitchen tabletop. She didn't say anything, didn't even ask any questions. But you could tell she was thinking by the way she narrowed her eyes as she stacked up some infants' rompers.

95

As Jen talked, the big old grandfather clock on the landing chimed four times, and in the living room, behind the sports page, surrounded by his duck-decoy collection (not to mention previously used juicers, lava lamps, and fondue pots), I knew my father was listening too.

For the second time that day I had found myself driving Jen Clinton away from an unsatisfactory and unsettling scene. This time her three enormous suitcases and a makeup bag the size of a Volkswagen were parked in my parents' hallway. Where else could I have taken her?

Not only was Jen my mom's favorite of my friends when we were little, she was, by Mom's calculations, a third cousin once removed of Captain Perk Ball's. When you're in trouble, family is everything on Beddoe's Island.

Being a celebrity soap diva didn't hurt either. Mom had had a million questions about a million different characters and story lines on *Hapless Hearts* that had to be plowed through before poor Jen could get to her real-life daytime drama.

"I need to know what happened to my mother," Jen concluded, back in real time. Once again she withdrew the brick from her handbag, placing it on my mother's clean table.

Mom wasted no time putting a paper towel under it before she examined it closely.

"Perk," she called to the living room. "Come here and look at this, willya?"

"It's a brick all right," my father pronounced, stroking his mustache the way he does when he's thinking. He picked it up and squinted at it. "Yeah," he finally said. "It's a brick."

96

But Mom was taking it very seriously. "Lookit that piece of wire, Perk. Where was the last place you saw a brick wrapped with wire like that?"

My father poured himself a cup from the coffeemaker that was eternally at the ready. He squinted at the brick, happy to be useful. "Way back there in the sixties when the Bayside Hotel burned down, there were all these old brick footers left. Well, we're poor people, but we're industrious, so we helped ourselves to them. You can see those old bricks all over the island. People built their steps with 'em, built their walkways, used 'em every which way they could. You can tell this one came from the hotel; it's got that glaze on it, that shiny glaze? Came from the old Watertown Brickyard." There is nothing my father enjoys more than talking about the old days on the Bay. You just have to stand back and let him rip; sooner or later he'll get to the point. "We used to use those bricks to weigh down the lids of the crab baskets those balsa-wood bushel baskets watermen use to carry their crabs? We fill 'em up, then mash a lid down on 'em, and twist the wires closed. Then sometimes we'd weigh down the top basket with a brick, wired to keep the lid closed on tight so the crabs didn't wiggle out. Sometimes we'd wire up a bunch of 'em together to use to mark our lays. See, you have your lay, then work your trotlines. You work up and down the line, takin' the crabs off your bait with a dip net as they come up over the roller up side of the boat. . . ."

I could tell that he'd lost Jennifer, but he went on for a while about the ins and outs of trotlining, the innate cussedness of crabs, and the vagaries of the crabber's life, just to hear himself talk. "The thing of it is, a waterman can find a hundred uses for a brick like this with a wire wrapped around it," he pointed out. "You

97

can mark your lay with a marker, see. You tie one end of a rope to the brick and the other end to a float, like a cork marker or an old Clorox jug, and you toss it overboard before you come in to mark where you were trotlining the previous day. When you come back out the next morning you look for your floats so you can crab in the exact same place. That's your lay, see?"

"Could you use this to weigh down the accelerator pedal of a car?" Jen asked.

My father considered this reluctantly. I could tell that he was as skeptical as I was about Jennifer's theory of foul play. "You could," he concluded at last. "But why would you want to?"

My mother leaned forward in her chair and frowned at the coffee mug in her hands. "I'd hate to think that someone killed poor Renata," she said at last. "Whatever she did, she didn't deserve that."

"What did she do?" Jen asked.

Mom picked up a fork and made several jabs into the remains of her strawberry pie. "It was a long time ago, honey. She was your mother. It's best to let sleeping dogs lie."

Jen looked to my father.

Dad pushed his hands deep into his pants pockets. He stared out the kitchen window, down toward the harbor.

"It's no good dredging all that stuff up again," he said distantly. "No one on the island wants to go through all of that again. You were raised by kind and decent folks, those grandparents of yours up there in New York. Let that be enough for you."

"You've got a wonderful career. Millions of people love Carla Devane. Why, you've even won Emmys, according to *Soap Opera Dish* magazine. Go forward, Jennifer, don't look back," my mother advised, patting her hand.

Jen and I exchanged a look. I shrugged, knowing nothing more than she did. She slumped back in her chair. "All these years of wondering what my mother was doing, where she was. I always felt incomplete. And now, not only did I find out my mother's dead, but my father's kicked me out of his house—and his life."

It would have wrung tears from a gargoyle.

I sipped my coffee, unimpressed but curious.

My mother finally cleared her throat.

"I have some old photo albums. Maybe you'd like to look at them." It was the thin end of the wedge.

Again I marveled at Jen's ability to bend people to her will.

It took some doing to move several boxes of old bridesmaids' dresses and tacky seventies plastic Christmas ornaments, but eventually, Mom was able to get into the bottom drawer of the desk.

"You all can help me take all this stuff down to the fire hall later on," she said as if she were offering us a rare treat.

"Remember when you and I would play dress-up from Miss Doll's rummage-sale boxes?" Jen asked me as she picked up an avocado-green sateen and tulle bridesmaid's dress and held it up to herself "Now people call these vintage clothes and pay a fortune for them!"

"I know there's a picture of you two in here somewhere, all dressed up in old Mrs. Bruckart's evening gowns." Mom pulled a stack of thick old albums out of the drawer and blew the dust off them.

We settled at the dining room table, pushing aside piles of polyester leisure suits and musty shag bath mats. "Now." My mother opened the first album, quickly flipping through the faded photographs. "No, this is too old; these are people I went to high school with. . . . Oh, my Lord, there's poor old Muriel Bruckart herself, speak of the devil, and your uncle Tummy, Holly. Actually, he was your great-great-uncle once removed on your grandfather's side. He used to roller skate to church every Sunday, but he died before you were born. He and old Mrs. Bruckart went to the old one-room schoolhouse down at Walnut Landing Wharf together. . . . Perk! Perk! Which album has all those old photos of the V.F.D. thirty-fifth-anniversary dinner at the Bayside? Oh, why ask him, he won't remember, men never do. . . ."

My father brought a slab of strawberry pie into the dining room to eat as he looked over my mother's shoulder. "Why, that's the old Bayside Hotel!" he exclaimed. "Remember when we used to go to the dances over there? Believe it or not, your mother and I could really cut a rug in the old days."

"We won some trophies, even. You two are too young to remember much about the Bayside, but it used to stand over to Shadbush Road. They had band come over there from Baltimore. It was quite the place in its day. People used to come from Washington and Baltimore and all over to stay there. Your Grandfather Russell used to carry gunning parties from there all winter."

Jen and I looked at the big white frame building in the faded sepia photograph. "It looks like a miniature Overlook Hotel." My observation was not meant to please and it did not.

"The Bayside was a grand place in its day," Dad defended it. "People would come from the city and stay there because it was cool; there was a breeze off the Bay there pret' near all the time."

"They had a good-size old ballroom in there too. Look, here's your aunt Tump and I all dressed up to go to one of those dances."

I studied the photograph of my mother and my aunt in their fifties dresses, with their Mamie Eisenhower hair and red lipstick, their long, full skirts, and enormous corsages pinned to their tight bodices. They were both younger than I am now.

"Oh, look how pretty you are there, Miss Doll!" It was just the sort of remark I'd expect from Jen. But it was true. In her late teens, marriage, motherhood, and forty years of fife's tribulations were still in the unknown future. My mother and my aunt gazed out at the camera, clearly delighted with themselves and their expectations.

"There's your dad when he'd just gotten back from Korea," Mom said, and I turned my gaze to the thin young man with the duck black hair, standing in someone's side yard in his army uniform, his forage cap jauntily tilted to one side, a cigarette held between his fingers. His eyes were shadowed as he gazed back at the camera, looking as if he had been interrupted on his way to somewhere else.

"How handsome you were, Mr. Perk." Jennifer gazed up at him adoringly.

"I thought I was something else," Dad admitted. "I'd just used my mustering-out pay to buy a workboat that day. I paid two hundred dollars for that boat. Albanus Mills made her, down to the Neck District."

Mom flipped through photos of graduations and Christmases and the faces of people who had died before I was born. I'd seen these photos before, but not for years, and not from this point of view.

"And, oh, where is it that I know I have some photos

of Renata and Busbee in here? Let's look at this album. Oh, *here's* your mother, in the early sixties," Doll told Jen, opening a green vinyl book decorated with smiley faces and happy daisies. "She came down here to work at the Bayside. She was the bookkeeper for the hotel when she met your father. A lot of places wouldn't hire women for jobs like that back then; she had to come all the way down here from Rochester just to work after she graduated from business college."

I bent over Jen's shoulder to study a snapshot of a dark-haired woman with big bouffant hair. She was standing proudly beside a reception desk, wearing white boots and a minidress in a bright lime green. She was heavily made up, with green shadow and long sweeps of black eyeliner extending from the outside corner of each eye. Her lips were a corpselike white. It was hard to tell behind the cosmetic mask, but if you looked twice you could see her resemblance to Jen. She was smiling, looking at the camera with a satisfied gaze and holding up her left hand to display a good-size diamond ring.

"That's her!" Jen bent over the photo, studying it closely. "Look at the size of that rock!"

"That was when she and your father got engaged," Mom said. "To think that we had those great big bouffant pageboy flips! We used to backcomb our hair and sleep with it wrapped in toilet paper to keep that look! That was the height of fashion back then, to look like Liz Taylor. We thought we were just so gorgeous. Your mother was so fashionable! She always had the most beautiful clothes. All the boys on the island were interested in her when she first came down to the Shore, but she picked out Busbee. He was different then. He was happier, not drinkin' so much, like he does now."

"That was back when your parents and us were all

friendly." My father was enjoying his memories. "We used to go around together quite a lot in those days, to all those dances and around to dinner and the Power Squadron and whatnot."

There were more pictures too. Photos of a young Busbee Clinton with a full head of hair and his arm around Renata, obviously proud of this beautiful young woman.

"Busbee was a whole lot different in those days. Dad cleared his throat. "He wasn't drinkin' so much then or . . . other things," he finished lamely, when he caught the speaking look my mother gave him. "We were all friends back then," he repeated.

There's no enemy quite as bitter as a friend who's betrayed you, I thought.

There were pictures of my parents and the Clintons together holding enormous drumfish. Sitting around a table piled high with empty crab shells. On a boat, where Renata held up a huge rockfish for the camera. Renata and Busbee standing beside a '58 fire-enginered Cadillac Coupe de Ville, grinning. The hand-lettered sign on the trunk said JUST MARRIED.

Then the pictures of my brother Robbie, a baby in Dad's lap, while Mom, enormously pregnant, smiled down at them, and then Jen and me in strollers, side by side, bundled up against the cold of a leafless winter landscape while our mothers, in their matching bouffants and stretch pants, proudly wheeled us down Island Road. Renata with a skunklike blond streak in her hair, a cigarette in one hand, looking up from a ledger book with her long red nails poised over the keys of an old-fashioned adding machine. Renata and Busbee in front of a Christmas tree, each one holding a snifter glass of Christmas cheer, toasting the camera. Busbee had the glassy look of someone who'd had several glasses of Christmas cheer.

Renata sitting on Santa's lap, in a bright red dress with a string of pearls around her neck. Her enormous mass of stiff dark hair almost obscured Santa's face. Then my mother, with her blond bouffant, in a maroon dress with the same Santa, laughing as she tweaked his red cap. Behind the fake beard and the red cap Santa's eyes looked familiar, but I couldn't place him.

Busbee and Dad cleaning fish, making faces. Busbee and Dad and Jack, the black Lab we used to have, standing in front of a shed wall covered with dead geese and ducks, their shotguns cradled in their arms. Snapshots of Jen and me, no more than three or four, in matching ruffled dresses. Jen and Robbie and I posed in Halloween costumes in front of our house. I was a Gypsy, Robbie was a cowboy, and Jen, naturally, was a princess. Jen and me in a series of dress-up clothes culled from Mom's rummage-sale boxes, looking like a pair of pint-size prostitutes with our smeared hubba-hubba red lipstick and blue eye shadow, but obviously just thrilled with ourselves. Jen and I in our children's choir robes at the church, clutching our junior hymnbooks, wanting to pretend that we were angels.

Renata, looking tense and distracted as she sat at a desk, stacks of ledger books piled up around her, a long thin strip of adding-machine tape in her hand. "All this nonsense about working mothers," Mom snorted. "Renata and I both worked right through our pregnancies and came back to work after we had our babies. We couldn't afford to stay home and be ladies of leisure back then!"

Busbee, caught by the camera unaware, holding a glass in his hand and looking startled, as if he'd been

104

snared in a shameful act. Renata and Busbee at a celebration somewhere, each one turned away from the other, lines of discontent and unhappiness in their expressions. Empty glasses, full ashtrays, and a wilted centerpiece filled the tablecloth in the foreground. In the back, two men in dinner jackets watched. The men looked familiar, but I couldn't place them either.

Last, there was Renata alone with her new beehive swirled up from her head like the topping on a Dairy Queen cone, smoking a cigarette and looking off into the distance as she stood beside the red Coupe de Ville. The lines of discontent that had begun to define her expression were set into place now. She had a harder, more jaded look about her as she avoided the eye of the camera. Inside the car, bundled up among the suitcases and boxes in the backseat, you could see Jen in a velvet beret and a car coat. No more than five or six, she pressed her face against the glass. It was, I guessed, the end of the marriage. "That was the day Renata left Busbee to go back to Rochester," my mother said. "See all the stuff packed up in the back?"

And then there were some loose eight-by-tens of a fire, then the burned-out shell of a building. Blackened rafters and chimneys rose from the rubble, soaring into a gray sky. "Perk, lookit that!" my mother exclaimed while Jen examined the photographs of her mother. "Here's some pictures of the Bayside fire! I don't remember those, do you?"

My father studied them for a minute. "Oh, that was a mess! The old frame hotel started blazing up in the middle of the night and was half burned up before we could get the fire trucks down there. It was the middle of the winter—in an ice storm, remember?—when most of the men were out with the dredge boats, oysterin', and we were shorthanded. Had to call to Marsh Ferry and Watertown for backup, but there wasn't much we could do. God, it was an awful night too. An ice storm, just like the night Renata went off the bridge—" He cut himself off and cleared his throat, nothing if not tactful.

"Oh, that was a terrible fire! That old place burned to the ground that night. It was a good thing it was the middle of the winter and closed up, so no one was killed." Mom sipped her coffee.

"That was when you had to start to feel sorry for Busbee." Dad sounded grudging. "His wife left him and took his kid, then his hotel burned down. After that he started to go downhill pretty bad, just got meaner and more and more miserly and miserable . . . ." He shook his head. "When I think that we were once friends . . ."

"Busbee owned the Bayside Hotel?" I asked.

Dad shrugged. "Well, he didn't own it all himself. He had two partners in it. Your father-in-law was one, and that chicken fella, Billy Chinaberry, he was the other. They pumped some money into that place after the war."

"It's the drink that made him turn mean," Mom said firmly. "Renata had to get away from him."

"H.P. and Billy Chinaberry were business partners with Busbee?" I found that hard to believe. I paged back through the album and found the photo of Busbee and Renata with the two strange men in the background. They were a young H.P. and a young Chinaberry. Had they ever been that age? I stared hard at the photo. The Old Man looked a lot like Sam back then, and it gave me a turn to recognize the father in the son.

"They were all in the war together. The Big One. They were all stationed in Europe at the same time, or something. I never did get the just right of it. Oh, yeah, they had some big plans for the Bayside. They were

106

gonna fix it all up and try to make it the way it had been when the steamboats brought the people over from Baltimore, back there around the turn of the century. Of course, back then none of them had the kind of money they have now, but they still had more than God."

"That was some night, when the hotel burned down," Mom continued, "I remember watching it from the bedroom window. You could see the flames all the way up here on Steamboat Road. You and Robbie were little, and I was so afraid that something would happen to your father down there. Oh, that was a fire. We've never had another one on the island like it. They thought someone had broken in and stolen some food or something, then just burned the place down by accident. Of course, by then, Jennifer, you and your mother were already gone, so you wouldn't remember that, but there's many a one on the island who recalls that night!"

"They put up those condos there where it used to be, back in the eighties," Dad informed us. He looked at the pictures again, shaking his head. "One of the boys on the V.F.D. got these from a newspaper photographer. We all got copies. You can see me down there in the corner by the pumper. Great God, it was cold that night! I froze on one side and fried on the other!"

"It wasn't much longer after that when your mother came back down to the island," Mom recalled as she looked at the old black and whites. "I saw her on the road, and she said she had some papers for Busbee to sign, then she was headin' back home, but she'd stop past. She never did though." My mother shook her head. "All these years, till last spring, I wondered what happened that she never did. I really couldn't imagine her running off and leavin' you. When you were a baby she dressed you up like a little doll and showed you off like you were Princess Poot. I could see why she left Busbee, why she chose to leave the Eastern Shore, but I didn't want to think that she could ever leave you."

"I've heard all the stories," Jen said, "about how people thought they saw her in Las Vegas or California. There was even an actress in a movie I saw once that looked like her, and I used to think that that was her, you know? And I always hoped she'd come back for me. But she never did. And now I know why. But I need to know how."

Mom reached over and touched her arm. "Sometimes you never know what really happened. It should be enough that you know that it was an accident, that she didn't abandon you. Believe me, Jennifer, I knew Renata as well as anyone, and I know, as true as I sit here, that she would never, ever go off and leave you. Ever."

Jennifer looked down at the photographs, a record of her mother's life on Beddoe's Island. She touched them with the tips of her fingers, then reached out for Mom.

"Maybe you're right," she said at last. "Maybe it was an accident."

But I was thinking about the Bayside Hotel, which I barely remembered from my childhood. It had seemed to me to be a place of vast open rooms and busy adults doing grown-up stuff. I could remember that Robbie and I were taken to the dining room for Sunday dinners every once in a while as a special treat, and how sophisticated and adult I felt sipping my Shirley Temple while my parents treated themselves to a rare cocktail. There were dim memories of running up and down the back halls there with Jen, and of Renata letting us play office with her adding machine.

"You've explained the connection between Busbee, H.P., and Billy Chinaberry to my satisfaction," I said.

108

"But the hotel they were partners in burned down thirty years ago. Do they still have business dealings with Busbee?"

"Who knows?" My father shrugged. "There was plenty of hard feeling to go around when the Bayside burned down, that's for certain."

"It stirred the pot considerably at the time," Mom said. "Of course, we heard Busbee had a lot less money invested in it than Wescott and Chinaberry, but he and Renata had a lot more to do with the running of it, until she left him. There were some stories—"

"What do you know about something called the Ornamental Hermit?" I asked.

Jennifer's cry was unexpected. It should have shattered all the glass in the china cabinet; all those struggling years in horror movies had given her a really piercing shriek. She was on her feet so fast that she knocked over her chair. Photos that my mother had been meaning to paste into albums for years flew across the dining room like wedding confetti. "Look!" She pointed to the front windows.

I saw the rhododendrons rustle, nothing more.

"I saw a man looking in the window!" Jen cried. "He was trying to get in!"

CHAPTER 10

A NOT FOR PROPHET ENDEAVOR

DAD RUSHED TO THE FRONT PORCH AND THREW THE door open. I was right behind him. Steamboat Road was empty; there wasn't as much as a bicyclist in sight in either direction. If anyone had been peering in the window they must have flown away on little pink wings.

Not even the neighbors were in their yards, although you'd think a scream like that would have brought them pouring out in hopes of some cheaper thrills than their own lives provided on a weekday afternoon. They must have been too engrossed in *Hapless Hearts* to care.

"Look around the house," Dad commanded, and we dutifully made a tour of the perimeter of the property. Not so much as a stray cat lurked under the porch. There wasn't a soul in the lilacs or even in the shed. Down past the garden the phragmites stood tall and still, so I knew no one had disappeared into the marsh or the shallow creek bed that separated us from the harbor.

"What did she see?" Dad panted, checking the backseat of Mom's car. "Who the hell are we looking for?"

"I didn't see," I gasped, loping up behind him. "I thought you did."

"Mmm!" My father frowned. "If there was anyone out here she scared 'em off with that scream. Damn if that girl don't have a pair of lungs on 'er!"

Ellery, turning his pickup into his driveway, avowed that he had not seen a soul on the road in either direction. "But you might check down to the bed and breakfast," he suggested. "Them goddamned tourists don't think nothin' 'bout comin' right up in the yard and walkin' right into yer house! T'other day Mertis and I was laying up in the bed, readin' the Sunday papers, and a whole pack of 'em marched right in the front door! You'd think the island was a goddamned historical park or some such shit!"

Ellery allowed as how the Preston boy, who had been taken up for peeping several years ago, was living in

Los Angeles, "where you can expect that kind of behavior from people." He was disappointed that we were not getting a posse organized to track down and kill any unsuspecting tourists, since there were so many men idled during the crab strike that a vigilante committee would be a welcome diversion.

Well, what he actually said was, "Damn if we don't need some excitement! Things have been right dull around here since the boys and them foreigner doctors from that bachelor party got into it over to the Bay Light about that stripper!"

"Too much time between hunting seasons for that one," my father grumbled after he had convinced Ellery that our celebrity guest was just fine, if perhaps a tad high-strung, as many celebrity persons were supposed to be.

When we tramped back into the house Jennifer was lying in the recliner in the living room with Mom taking her pulse and looking concerned.

She well might have; Jen was hyperventilating, and her face was blue. "I . . . I . . . looked up and I . . . I saw him," she gasped when we returned empty-handed. "I thought it was the stalker!"

Again I suspected that the line between Jen and Carla was crumbling around the edges. "The stalker?" I repeated.

Jen nodded and sat up. When she looked at me I could see the whites of her eyes. "That's *really* why they put me on hiatus at the show. This . . . this *man* has been following me, harassing me. *Threatening* me. Network security hasn't been able to figure out who he is yet, so they suggested that I leave Manhattan for a while. I never thought he'd find me down here!" She collapsed back in the chair, eyes closed, while Mom

111

made little fussing noises.

"Why didn't you tell me about this earlier?" I was a mite pissed. "That's one hell of a thing to spring on people!"

Jen shook her head. "I was afraid," she said, opening her eyes. "You don't know what it's like! It took me forever to convince the producers and security that I wasn't imagining this, that it was really happening. And I thought if I was written off the soap for a while, maybe he'd get bored and go away. He just follows me everywhere. To and from work, to stores, to the theater—everywhere! But I never thought he'd find me down here!" She burst into tears.

"Oh, for God's sake, Jen. Get a grip," I snapped. "Who is this alleged stalker? What's his MO.? Why didn't you say something to Friendly when we were out at the barracks? Shouldn't you have let local law enforcement know immediately if someone's pursuing you?"

Jen looked up at me from tearstained eyes. Her mascara was running. She looked like a demented Bambi. "How could you?" she demanded. "You don't believe me?"

"*I* saw something out there!" My mother, ever the protective lioness, sprang to the defense of her favorite soap heroine in distress. And I had to admit that Jen did distress very well. You could barely tell she was acting.

"She says there was a face," Perk said. He glared at me.

"Oh, for God's sake," I sighed. "Okay, I think I saw something too, if it makes you feel any better. Is this really why you came down here?"

"He's probably somewhere on the island right now," Jen whispered between chattering teeth. "Just waiting

112

for me!" She moaned softly.

"There isn't a man staying down at the bed and breakfast," Dad said as he hung up the phone. "They say they're filled up with the Dundalk Lesbian Bicycling Association!"

"Should we call the po-lice? Or better yet, call Cal and tell him to raise the drawbridge! That way no one can get off the island!" Mom was ready to woman the barricades.

"Did you actually see a face at the window?" I asked Mom.

"Well, no," she admitted. "But Perk saw it, didn't you, honey?"

"I saw something," he said uncertainly.

"He's out there," Jen moaned. "He's found me somehow."

"What does this stalker do, Jen? How does he operate?"

"He follows me. Everywhere I go, there he is."

"But does he do anything? I mean, does he try to talk to you, phone you up and breathe, or touch you or send you dead flowers through the mail or anything?"

"No, nothing like that. He's just always there! That's why it's so hard to get security to press charges! He never does anything! He's just always there!" Her voice slid into a whine. "I mean, this is Manhattan, not the island. There are eight million people! You just can't always be *there* where I am by accident. Oh, he's stalking me all right!"

Call me mean, call me evil, but remember, I'd just chased around the house looking for something or someone I wasn't even sure was there. "Why would he want to stalk you?"

Jen gave me a sharp, offended look. "Because of

113

Carla. These people have no lives except what they see on the soaps, and it all gets twisted up and evil in their minds, and they decide that they have a relationship with you, that they own you somehow. It happens to us famous people all the time! One actress had to leave the business because she was being stalked! Another actress was *killed* by a stalker!" Jen glared at me. "This is not a joke, Holly! It's really not!"

"You poor dear!" Mom was all sympathy. "What a terrible thing! Well, if there's a stranger on the island, believe me, folks'll know about it soon enough, and everyone will keep an eye on him!"

"They do that with all the visitors," I pointed out in what I thought was a reasonable voice. "The ones they don't cook and eat."

"Don't you make fun of this island! You were born and bred among these people, and you're no better than anyone else around here!" My father was getting huffy, which he does when he's nervous.

Forgive me if I was cynical. Stalkers were currently in fashion; there was a deranged-maniac-is-following-me-around-story line on every talk show, every movie of the week, and every soap that season. It had just replaced the national sick fascination with "recovered memory" syndrome, which in turn had replaced the Satanic day-care hysteria. Jen's self-dramatization was just too . . . well, *timely* to suit me, too much a thing of the moment, like her Versace suit. I'm not saying people don't get stalked or abused in real life; I'm just saying that real agony is cheapened when it becomes the misery of the week.

But Perk and Doll were TV watchers and true believers. "You two are a pair of crisis queens who love nothing more than a drama," I said wearily. "Give you

114

half a rumor that it's going to rain tomorrow, and you're calling for the second Deluge!"

Wrong thing to say.

"Well!" My mother feathered up. "That's a fine way to talk to your own parents, who sweated blood so that you could go to college and waste your life marrying that miserable playboy and becoming a reporter for that miserable paper where they don't pay you enough to buy a decent car!"

Dad was right behind her. "When all them ol' cops was after you for murdering Jason Hemlock, I'd like to know who got you off the island?" he demanded.

"I've got to call my agent," Jennifer said, struggling to rise from the depths of the recliner.

"Your agent?" I was surprised, to say the least. "You say you're being stalked by a crazed lunatic and you want to call your agent? That's entertainment! Call the cops!"

"No, don't do that," Jen begged. "The publicity would get me fired! I'm on short notice as it is!"

Mom shook her head mournfully. "Jennifer's your oldest friend and she's in trouble with some maniac, and all you can do is act like you don't care!"

"Is this a publicity stunt?" I demanded. "Because if it is—"

"Don't be a smartmouth," my father said.

"It's a terrible trauma!" Jen exclaimed.

"And a little something you didn't bother to mention," I replied. She looked away, and I wondered what other little secrets she was stashing away.

"You don't know what I've been through these past six months," Jen said, tears glittering. "If you had to go through life without your mother—"

"If that is indeed why you're here. Why don't you

want to call the police? Why didn't you think to mention this stalker before? Jen, is this some kind of publicity stunt or something?" My reporter sense was tingling.

"Please, Holly. I'm on edge as it is now." Jen collapsed back into the recliner. "I'm under so much stress."

"Look, all I asked was—"

"That's enough, Hollis." My father turned on me. "Why are you always so cynical? Look at the poor girl! Stop tormenting her!"

"But I—"

"Maybe you need to have more sympathy for the problems of others," Mom sniffed. "Poor Jennifer, you can tell us all about it while I fix us all another cup of coffee and another piece of my strawberry pie."

"Nothing for me," I said between clenched teeth. "I have to go out and find a new job and a nice man and reproduce now."

"Don't talk to your mother like that," Dad said.

"If you can't be civil, then maybe you'd better leave," Mom haughtily commanded me.

"Fine! I think I can do that!" I said.

I left the three of them to dramatize what had no doubt been nothing more than a bird in the bush, which was worth more than a strawberry pie in the hand.

I hate it when Mom and Dad start up with me. Sometimes I think if Adolf Hitler came by they'd side with him over me.

On my way out I almost slammed into Mertis and Ellery on their way in with a plate of fried soft crabs.

"I just thought Carla would like some real good homemade seafood," Mertis said, craning her neck to see around me.

"She's our favorite TV star," Ellery explained. "We jes' love little Carla."

"If she's in trouble the whole island will want to know," Mertis explained, ready to burst her bladder at the mere idea of contact with an Actual Celebrity. And they would find out real soon too. She's not known as the "Beddoe's Island Gazette" for nothing. By dinnertime Jen would be up to her eyeballs in coffee cake, crabs, and autograph seekers. She could tell 'em all any damned story she wanted too. I was past caring.

If Rig wanted a story he could get it himself.

I left the island in a snit, and damned glad to get out of there too.

Something was wrong, but I didn't know what.

"These people are too crazy even for me, and I am one of them, so what does that make me?"

"That makes you a world-class fool," Sam replied. He was sitting on the glider on the screened porch, with Venus, the Cat with an Attitude, snuggled up beside him, purring in ecstasy as his ghostly fingers scratched her ears. Me, she couldn't care less about. For her, I'm eat, sleep, in, out.

"Yeah, but . . . it just doesn't feel right. I think it's all some kind of publicity stunt," I replied morosely.

The funny thing about Sam is that I may not see him for weeks, and I'll think he's gone, and then he'll just suddenly start haunting me again. In that sense—and that sense only—he's a lot like God: He's never there when I call him, but he's always on time.

I was so happy to have him there to pick over the whole stalker mess with me that I broke open a brand-new bag of Reese's Peanut Butter Cups. I also realized that I had not thought about cigarettes for several hours, which was another good reason to celebrate.

Sam doesn't exactly eat or drink. It's more like he sort of *inhales* the essence of worldly goodies. I can always tell when he's been sneaking my Reese's; they taste oddly flat because he's sucked the chocolate peanut butter-ness out of them. If he could suck the calories, cholesterol, and fat out of food, we could make a fortune and I could retire, but things don't work out that way.

"I don't understand why you're so pissed off that she didn't tell you about the stalker. After all, doesn't every celebrity have one? And maybe she is right. Maybe someone did kill Renata." Sam leaned back into the glider and contemplated the spring evening.

Down in the woods behind my house, the peepers had begun their spring song. A fingernail moon hung over the pines. Warm weather was almost on us. The daffodils were almost finished, and the first scent of the lilacs coming in was just noticeable in the air. Across the fields the headlights on my landlord's tractor came on, illuminating his turned-up soybean fields. The loamy smell of fresh earth hung in the air.

"Yeah, but it makes me wonder what else she's not telling me," I complained. "I feel like a chump. I feel *manipulated* No one likes that."

"No, of course not. *Malaise tout comprendre, c'est tout pardonner, non?*"

"Sorry, I didn't have a prep-school education, just four years of high-school French," I said nastily.

"Several prep schools," Sam laughed. "I kept getting thrown out for one thing or another, so the Old Man would have to endow a gym or a new library somewhere else so I could complete my alleged education—"

"That reminds me of something I forgot to mention!" I interrupted him. "You'll never guess who I saw today!"

"I hate gossip," Sam replied with a straight face. "Who?"

"Your father! The Old Man himself! And he was with Billy Chinaberry!"

"My father?" Sam frowned. "Boy, you're in bad company, aren't you?"

"Talk about your unresolved issues—and we were—I don't understand why you don't haunt him. You two had more hostility going on than the Six Day War, and—"

Sam's outline glowed in the dimming light. "Never mind all that," he said shortly. "What was he doing?"

"Well, right before Busbee told Jen not to darken his door again, the Old Man and Billy Chinaberry showed up chez Clinton."

"So the Poultry Prince hasn't used up his obit yet?"

"No, but he looked really gray and sick. Anyway, they wanted to know about the Ornamental Hermit, whatever that is. So then, when we were looking through the old albums, Mom and Dad told me that your father and Chinaberry and Busbee were army buds who went into partnership on the old Bayside Hotel thirty years ago, and that it burned down right after Renata blew out of Dodge."

Sam stretched by rising a few inches in the air off the glider cushions. "Wouldn't surprise me one bit. It seemed like the Old Man always had his fingers in everything in those days. Of course, my sister and I were in boarding schools, so we weren't around to witness the fun."

"It's an interesting connection, I think." I bit into a

119

Reese's Cup.

"Ah! You said you had washed your hands of this whole thing!" Sam cocked his head.

"That doesn't mean I'm not interested. What is the Ornamental Hermit? Can you use your ghostly powers to find that out?"

"Whaddya think I am, the Internet?" Sam asked. He thought for a moment. "A yard statue, maybe, like one of those gnomes?"

"Maybe. But why would that bother them after all these years?"

"Say, not that I care or anything, but how did the Old Man look?" Sam's voice was just a shade too casual.

"As much like a Big Daddy in a bus-and-truck tour of *Cat on a Hot Tin Roof* as ever. All he needs is an ice cream suit. He's already got the power trip down."

"What a pisser the Old Man is," Sam chuckled. He almost sounded fond of his father, something that could only have happened over his own dead body.

"My, you are mellowing out in your old age," I laughed.

"Aw," Sam muttered. "It's not like I actually *care* or anything."

"Actually, I would have to say that you care a great deal," drawled a soft voice from the corner of the porch. It was more like the rush of wind in the pines or water lapping at the tide line than a human voice, rich with the cadences of the South. "Troubled relationships between fathers and sons is something we both know about, right, Sammy?"

"Ed, I thought I told you never to call me here." Sam, suddenly sulky, slumped down into the glider cushions, shoving his hands into his pants pockets like a thwarted teenager. "Oh, man!"

"Exactly." The voice chuckled, and a form began to take shape in a battered old lawn chair no one ever sat in if they could help it. I watched as the black formal clothes came together, then the delicate hands and feet, and then the dark eyes and the broad forehead beneath a crown of unruly black hair.

"Edgar Allan Poe?" I squeaked. "Sam, Edgar Allan Poe is sitting in an aluminum lawn chair right on my porch!" I went to clutch Sam's arm, but, of course, my hand passed right through him.

"Well, dear lady," the revered revenant drawled, bowing in my direction, "let us say the *shade* of Poe is here. Sorry, I don't have a *carte de visite,* but it is me, nonetheless. Or should I say *I*? The rules of grammar have changed so much in the past one hundred and fifty years . . ."

"What are you doing here?" Sam grumbled. "No one invited *you*."

"Uninvited, but not, I trust, unwelcome to our hostess?" Poe crossed his ankles. He was so small that his feet barely touched the floor; I had to remind myself that he was of a more diminutive generation.

"Mr. Poe, this is such an honor, I mean, I am one of your biggest fans! Except for my friend Judge Carroll, who named his pet crow after you. I mean . . ." I was gushing like a fountain and unable to stop as I sank myself deeper and deeper into obsequious, fawning embarrassment. "I mean, the last thing I expected was one of the greatest American writers on my porch—"

"He's here because he's my sponsor in G.A.," Sam sighed.

"Ghosts Anonymous." Mr. Poe nodded. "And you know our credo, Sammy. That's why they call it Anonymous."

121

"Yeah, yeah, yeah," Sam sulked.

"And as surprising as it may seem, this isn't about you," Mr. Poe added, "although we have missed you at the meetings lately."

"I've been busy," Sam muttered.

"Oh, we know that," Mr. Poe replied cheerfully. "We're ready to deal with your issues whenever you are." He turned to address me. "It's always a pleasure to meet a fellow writer, Ms. Ball."

"Oh, but I'm just a reporter; I'm not a real writer like you, Sir," I giggled, helpless in the clutches of my own celebrity awe. "Not a genius."

Oh, please, I tried to command my mouth, stop running, just shut up. But my tongue had detached itself from my brain. "You've always been one of my favorite writers, a seminal influence on my decision to become a writer. I mean, you are . . . were a genius! I just wish you could see the way they've enshrined you, every schoolchild, Roger Corman, Vincent Price. . . I mean, in Baltimore alone, they've . . . made you a god. When I was a kid they took us all up to your grave at Westminster . . ."

Please, mouth, just be still, I prayed. But my verbal diarrhea just got worse and worse and worse. "I just can't tell you what a great honor this is. I mean, Sam never told me he knew you, but I guess the Rules, you know, say he can't talk about famous friends or something. . . . Wow, I mean, I'm like one of your biggest fans!"

Mr. Poe made a gesture that expressed his modesty. But he was a writer; you could tell he was enjoying a healthy helping of homemade flattery.

"He's just here because I've missed a couple of meetings, that's all," Sam interjected. "Okay, okay, so I had a slip! Sue me!"

Poe gazed at him sadly, as only a man with those huge dark eyes could gaze with great and mournful sorrow. "Sam, I am not here about your . . . ah, slip. I'm here because this lovely flower of southern womanhood needs some direction."

"Yeah, yeah, yeah. It's real convenient, isn't it? My father's name comes up and here you materialize on Holl's porch because she needs some 'direction.' "

"Actually, Sammy, it would seem that your father is not the only mortal with whom you have issues. Your relationship with Miss Ball is a topic of interest—"

"Hey! Don't even go there!" Sam yelped.

Mr. Poe's hands came up; he touched the tips of his fingers together. He raised one eyebrow expressively. "Sometimes I think you're a little too in touch with your inner child, Sammy," he said in a gentle voice. "I assure you that my visit, unannounced though it might be, is strictly to assist Ms. Ball. As you know, the Rules specifically state in Addendum Seventeen, Volume Three, Book Eight, Chapter Four, Paragraph Twenty-seven—"

"Hollis doesn't want to hear all that," Sam snapped.

"Oh, but I do!" I said. "I want to hear anything that Mr. Poe has to say! He can sit here and recite the Santimoke-Devanau Counties Phone Book if he wants!" I tried to strike a pose that would convey rapturous interest in every word Poe uttered. I probably just looked as if I were working a crick out of my neck, but I was too enraptured to care.

"Can I offer you a Reese's Cup?" I asked. "Diet Pepsi? It's caffeine-free," I added in my new idiot's voice.

"No, no, thank you, dear lady," Poe chuckled. "No

mortal sustenance for me, I thank you. Unless you happen to have some pecan divinity fudge on hand?"

"Uh, no, but I think I've got some beer in the back of the refrigerator."

Poe gave me a wounded look. "My proclivity for spirits, I assure you, is a vile canard, put about by my literary rivals. As is my addiction to opiates, I might add. Like so many other lies that have dogged my steps." He sighed. "Penury, obscurity, poverty, foul editors, unspeakable publishers . . . but as a writer you are familiar with all of that." I could only nod.

But Mr. Poe was especially interested in my agreement. He inhaled deeply of the spring evening. "When I was alive, we—dear Virginia, Muddie, and I—starved and froze! I was mocked and cheated! Paid a pittance! Worse, my work was all but ignored by an ignorant and philistine public." He shook his head. "And now that I am dead I'm a bloody industry!"

"Oh, put a sock in it, Ed!" Sam suggested nastily. "We've all heard the starving-writer slash underappreciated-artist thing before!"

"Someone published a psycho-biography of me this year," Poe fumed "A psycho-biography! Pah! He got more of an advance for this shriveled-up pack of speculations and half-truths than I received for my entire body of work!"

"No!" I breathed. "That is, I can believe that!"

"Writers not fit to wipe Judith Krantz's pen have gotten tenure at prestigious universities with their dreary little papers on why I was kicked out of West Point! Vampires! And they think that *I* wrote horror stories!"

His shade bounced up and down in the lawn chair with excitement, and his pale face was turning scarlet-unless it was the reflection of the setting sun on his ectoplasm.

"What's your point, Ed?" Sam demanded.

"Shh," I hissed at him.

"Well, you haven't heard all this a hundred times, and I have," he muttered.

"Not that I'm complaining about being famous. It's just that when I was alive I couldn't get arrested, and now that I'm dead they're crawling all over me! Where were all these people when I was starving? When Sissie was dying? That's what I need to know!"

I had no answer.

"Cut to the chase, Ed," Sam said in a flat voice. "We've got unfinished business here."

Poe drew in a long breath, stared hard at Sam, then released it. "Forgive me, dear lady," he said. "You must understand that I need a moment to restore myself." He closed his eyes and became utterly still. Then, as we watched, he began to shrink.

Slowly, he grew smaller and smaller and smaller, until it seemed as if he was a tiny black dot, no larger than a spider, suspended in the empty air above the chair.

"Cheap ghost tricks," Sam remarked, but I had the feeling that he wished he could make himself a black dot like that. Probably it took years of practice and the sort of concentration Sam's Zippy-on-speed mind simply couldn't achieve, but that's just my guess.

There was a thin, whispery sound, and slowly Mr. Poe seemed to inflate himself until his canescent form filled the chair again.

"Sorry about that. Where are my manners?" he fretted as he adjusted his neckcloth and picked invisible specks of lint from his frock coat. "Forgive me, dear lady. As you can see I have some unresolved issues of my own.

As a writer I am sure that you can comprehend my distress."

"Oh, please don't think anything of it," I said quickly, ever the gracious hostess.

Poe shot his cuffs. "Since evening is almost upon us I should come to the point of my visit," he sighed. "If I could just remember what it was."

The three of us—myself and two ghosts—sat in silence on the screened porch for several moments while the great man recollected himself

Finally, Mr. Poe placed a finger against his luxuriant mustache and began to stroke it thoughtfully. His small feet, encased in polished black boots, tapped at the empty air above the porch floor.

"Oh, yes, now I recall," he sighed. "You, dear lady, had a question that no one in the depressingly technological times you live in seemed to be willing or, may I say, able to answer." He sounded a trifle smug, I had to admit. "So much of what was once gracious and charming in life seems to have fallen by the wayside, including the fine art of gardening."

"Well, I have a couple of tomato sets I keep meaning to put in, and my mother has some really nice plantings around her house," I offered. "But—"

Poe held up a hand. "No, no, no. I am aware that even in these times of the downsized discretionary income, there are still those who have the means and the inclination to pursue the dreams of the garden as it was envisioned by Capability Brown and William Kent. I speak, dear lady, of the great estate gardens of the eighteenth and nineteenth centuries. Whole acres of beautifully laid out grounds, mind you, with formal gardens and statuary and beautiful, beautiful plantings. Such luxuries are still not completely unknown in this

126

ugly technological century, I believe, although most are now in public hands?"

"He's talking about places like Ladew Topiary Gardens and Longwood," Sam put in helpfully. "Those big formal gardens?"

"I knew that," I said. Even if I had been a little hazy on the concept, I would have preferred a hysterectomy with a rusty spoon to admitting my ignorance to Sam.

"In the eighteenth century," Poe rhapsodized, "such gardens were a part of every English stately home. In that time there was a rage for Gothic ruins to go with one's Italian fountains and Greco-Roman statuary. If the estate had no ruined monastery on the premises, well, the nobleman would have one built, to give him a vista to look at from the terrace of his great house. *That* was the great age of gardens." Mr. Poe sighed.

"Cut to the chase, Ed," Sam suggested again. "Holl doesn't have all night, you know. She's still a mortal, although she could be dead of old age by the time you finish."

"Shh," I told him. "Please, Mr. Poe, continue."

Poe bowed in my direction. "Thank you, dear lady. I shall sum up my tale shortly, and as you shall see, all the back story that has gone before will be necessary to the point of the narrative."

"Please proceed, Sir," I returned his bow with one of my own. "You were telling us about the great age of gardens."

"Ah, yes. As I was trying to say." Poe gave Sam a flat look. "The truly fashionable gardener wanted a novelty on his property. And if he didn't have an authentic pile of stones, he would have a, shall we say, reproduction ruin built."

I nodded to show that I was listening.

127

"As I am sure you have studied in your English literature classes, there was a great passion for the Gothic, the medieval, the supernatural, and the outlandishly fanciful. It was this passion that inspired my own writings." He coughed modestly. "You might have thought this passion would culminate in the fake ruin. But no, human nature being what it was, the temptation to gild the lily proved irresistible. Thus, it became *de rigueur* to create a hermitage and actually install a man in it to add perspective to the landscape. As well as a touch of romance. The man's job was to be purely decorative. And of course he had to have some romantic, moldy sort of aura. And thus was born one of the oddest occupations in history, that of the ornamental hermit."

If I had been nodding off before, I was wide awake now. "Did you say the Ornamental Hermit?" I demanded.

"I said the ornamental hermit," Mr. Poe affirmed. "His job was to sit in a *faux* hermitage all day long and look like a hermit. Queen Caroline had such a hermit at Richmond. His name was Stephen Duck, and he was a self-taught poet. He allowed his hair and nails to grow in order to look the part. How long he and his compeers sat in their faux hermitages is not recorded. Duck did rather well by his job; he became rector of Byfleet and mayor of the eponymous Duck Island, in the middle of St. James's Park. It was very much in the spirit of the age, you know, if a trifle decadent. Unfortunately, human hermits were always sneaking off to the local pub, or smuggling their wives in, so eventually, they had to resort to stuffed hermits. Duck drowned himself in the Thames . . . ." He smiled at me encouragingly.

"So an ornamental hermit is someone who sits in a

fake hermitage in some rich English guy's enormous garden and pretends to be a real hermit, just for looks."

"Exactly!" Mr. Poe beamed at me.

"A living lawn gnome!" Sam exclaimed happily.

I pressed my fingers against my temples. I could feel a headache coming on. If Poe wasn't one of the greatest writers in the English language, I would have accused him of making this all up.

"What did you write under Occupation on your tax return?" Sam asked. "*Ornamental hermit?*"

Poe tsked. "What do they teach young people these days?" he asked rhetorically.

"They teach them to read Poe," Sam said. "Believe me, I had to read all your stuff."

"And precious little good it did you," Mr. Poe retorted. "Your wit is primitive, your manners barbaric, and your haunting skills are crude at best." He sniffed.

"Can I trade him in for you?" I asked. Well, hope does spring eternal.

"Unfortunately, no, dear lady." Mr. Poe laughed.

"Next time I'm telling Shemp Howard to make an appearance," Sam threatened. "Now, there's a fun ghost! Nyuck, nyuck, nyuck!"

"Let me get this straight. An ornamental hermit's whole job was just to sit there and look decorative."

Poe leaned back in his chair. "It was the Italian influence, you see. They all went on the Grand Tour in those days, to France and Italy, and picked up their landscaping tips from the climes of Naples and Rome. When you add the literary passion of the age for the Middle Ages, knights and monasteries, vampires, and, ahem, ghosts—"

"For which," Sam said wearily, "you can thank those two Brit jerks Byron and Shelley. Boy, there's a pair of assho—"

"—and the relatively cheap cost of labor in those days, and the conspicuous consumption of the rich—"

"You come up with an Ornamental hermit," I concluded. "But what does a fake recluse from the seventeen hundreds have to do with Busbee Clinton, Billy Chinaberry, and H. P. Wescott?"

Poe inclined his head to one side, smiling as he regarded me with his enormous, melancholy eyes. Slowly, his form began to fade away, blending with the lengthening shadows and gathering darkness.

"That, dear lady," he said, as his voice turned to the whisper of the wind in the pines, "is not the question you asked. You wanted to know what an ornamental hermit was, and I told you . . . ."

And with a fading bow he was gone. The empty chair stood in the corner of the porch as it always had. Not even the dust was disturbed.

"I guess that saved me a lot of library time," I turned to say to Sam, "but I still don't understand why—"

But Sam was gone too.

So I sat alone in the long darkness of spring, thinking my own thoughts. One question was answered, but all it had done was lead to a thousand more. And I'd forgotten to get Poe's autograph.

CHAPTER 11

BAD COMPANY

THAT'S THE TROUBLE WITH SIGNS AND OMENS AND haunts. They never seem to give you any sort of information you can really use, like the winning lottery number for next Tuesday or what really happens to the socks you lose in the wash. Oh, no. They just show up and prose on and on about seventeenth century gardens, or they drag you into their problems.

By Wednesday I was more than ready to abandon the Ornamental Hermit, Jen Clinton, Renata Ringwood, and the whole entire mess to whatever fates there were. As thrilling as it was to get a visit from Edgar Allan Poe, the distinguished dead author hadn't really been a whole lot of practical help.

Great genius of American literature or not, it seemed to me that Mr. Poe was in a position to tell me a lot more than he did, and I was sort of resenting that.

Wednesday was not a day made for such ruminations. I'd spent my morning in a stiffing, overheated courtroom as the lawyers ran up their hourly rates yammering on, while through the open window I could see the beautiful spring day beckoning me outside. It would have been a great day to plant my tomatoes. Or just lie on a blanket with a book in the sun. I watched while Edgar Allan Crow, the courthouse's resident bird, perched on the windowsill and took a look at the proceedings, then flew away with a caw of disgust.

When Judge Carroll finally declared a lunch recess I bought a hot dog and a bag of chips, settling myself on one of the benches in the courtyard for a brief hour of warm sunlight and blooming trees.

My bullshit detector should have gone up when I saw no one other than H. P. Wescott striding up the brick walkway. I took a bite of my hot dog and hoped I was invisible.

But no; the Old Man stopped right in front of me, his heavy eyebrows drawn together like two thunderclouds. "I want a word with you," he said tightly. He loomed

131

over me like an Old Testament prophet.

My hot dog turned to a lump of clay in my mouth. That man sure knew how to ruin my good time. "Well," I said with my mouth full, "look who's here. The life and death of every party."

"Now, you look here, Hollis," he said, pointing a big blunt finger at me. "I don't know what you and that Clinton girl are up to, but I'm warning you right now." The finger stabbed at the air in front of my face. "You stay out of my business, you hear? I won't have it!"

His finger looked like a hot dog, I thought. A big red hot dog. I could have reached out and taken a bite, it was that close to me. "Which business is that, H.P? The Bayside Hotel? The Ornamental Hermit? Renata Ringwood Clinton? Fill me in so I can avoid it."

His heavy face suffused with color so that he turned a bright purple. "You, you . . ." he started to say.

"H.P., think about your blood pressure," I reminded him. Truth to tell, I didn't want him to keel over right there with another heart attack. When you find a worthy opponent you don't want to lose him.

"You just stay away from the whole thing!" He looked down at me from his great height. "I'm warning you, Hollis. Stay away from the Ornamental Hermit! It's none of your business. And keep that actress away from it too! You hear me?"

"What's the Ornamental Hermit?" I asked.

H.P. gave me a foul look. Without another word he turned and walked away. I watched as he climbed into his Mercedes and spun out into the noonday traffic on Chesapeake Street.

I'd been warned, but about what? Somehow, whenever the Old Man tried to warn me away from something, I always hit pay dirt.

I bit into my hot dog.

It was a dark and stormy night.

No, I swear, it really was.

That night I had a strange dream.

A clap of thunder awoke me from a deep sleep with the idea that there was an old, stale cigarette under the sofa. I could almost see it. Still in a coma, I got out of bed and stumbled through the dark down the stairs.

My house was pitch black when I staggered downstairs, and no amount of flicking switches or cursing brought the power back up. So, I groped in the cold darkness and managed to fall over my own furniture only once or twice before I could see well enough to load some damp wood into the stove and start a fire to take the edge off the night chill.

As I stood in front of the blazing iron box and shivered, half-awake, I sleepily reflected upon those terminally cute photographs of quaint, antique country decor one sees in the glossier shelter magazines, and thought if someone *made* those people live that eighteenth-century lifestyle without power and plumbing or even a decent dish soap, they'd file a class-action suit.

Since my tenant farmhouse was more likely to be featured in *Circumstances of the Poor and Obscure* than *Architectural Digest*, this would not be a problem for me in the foreseeable future. Wind was seeping through every ancient nook and crack, shaking at the windows and moaning at the door, making the firelight gutter, casting weird shadows across the walls.

It was a good night for a murder, I thought as I dropped to my hands and knees by the couch, groping among the dust kitties and forgotten pencils for that elusive cigarette. In my dim state I could almost taste it.

And that was when there was a clang in the kitchen, as if the dishes in the drainer had shifted.

It must be Venus, I thought, and continued my groping.

Who else, I wondered irritably, would be running around on a night like this?

Then I remembered that Venus was outside. She loves weather like this. A flash of lightning illuminated the room, casting familiar objects into threatening shadows.

I heard the unmistakable sound of a car engine starting.

I peered out the window, but all I saw was a pair of glowing red taillights disappearing down the lane in the rain.

At that moment Venus began to yowl at the door, so I let her in, then stumbled back upstairs to bed, still comatose.

In the morning I decided that I had dreamed it all.

But at least I didn't smoke that cigarette.

CHAPTER 12

CATCH OF THE DAY

FRIDAY NIGHT ON THE WATER STARTED OUT BEAUTIFULLY. Twilight and tide were both coming on. Everyone was in a let's-have-a-couple-of-beers-and-fish mode, which suited me fine. I cast my line and sat on the stern board, half listening to the Guy Talk Show, with your hosts Orm Friendly and Toby Russell.

"Maybe we should move over to the other side. It

looks like that guy in that aluminum skiff is catching something over there, huh? Whaddaya think?"

"I dunno. We're right over the rocks here. Why move? Tide's turning; they'll be biting soon. *Uuuuuuuuurrrrp*. You wan' another beer?"

"Will you guys shut up? You'll scare the fish."

"What fish? There ain't nothin' bitin' out here."

"Them boys come in the bar said they caught a couple good-size rock out here last night. One weighed seven pounds."

When I was just about old enough to coordinate myself, Dad put a fishing pole into my hands and took me out on the boat, just as he had done with Robbie before me. From the minute I cast my first line into the deep green waters of Chesapeake Bay, I was hooked on fishing, and I still am to this day.

Just as Venus will arouse herself from a coma to respond to the sound of the can opener, all I need to hear is the sound of a reel spooling some twenty-pound test mono, and I'm there.

I'm not much for the expensive fancy tackle I see a lot of fishermen invest in. You can keep your graphite rods and your three-hundred-dollar Shakespeare reels; I'm still fishing on the same green Fiberglas rod my dad gave me for my tenth birthday, and I don't know who made my reel, but I think my father won it in a domino game over to Omar Hinton's store in Oysterback. As long as I keep it cleaned and oiled, it seems to work just fine for me and for the rockfish and blues I like to catch. I've got my tackle box with my bucktails and spinners and Day-Glo surgical eels, the lead sinkers and handmade lures and Just Rite hooks and the Buck knife that used to belong to my grandfather; these are the magic charms for lucky fishing. Call me up and I am good to go. The smell of saltwater and gasoline is perfume to me. And fishing is balm to my stressed-out soul.

Which was why I couldn't understand why Friendly and Toby were so bent out of shape that they just weren't biting that Friday night. While there's nothing quite like the strike of a seven-pound rock to get your adrenaline going, I don't really care if I catch a fish or not.

It's the being there that I like: the sound of the tide slapping against the hull, the gentle rocking of the boat, the openness of the water, the lucid, pungent smell of salt and peeler and fuel. It's the feel of the wind across the waves, the warmth of the afternoon sun sinking behind the trees, casting darkness across the water that warmed my bones after the long winter And the connection between my soul and my hook, that thin silver fine of monofilament a manifest link between my spirit and nature—I like that too. There's a great sense of peace you get when you cast your line off the Swann's Island light, put your mind on idle, and wait for something shimmering and invisible beneath the water to take your bait, give you that strike that will send the excitement pulsing through your whole body as you begin to reel in your catch.

It's the word made fish, and I love it.

Catching fish is nice, but really not necessary. After a week of witnessing humanity at its worst, a warm April evening spent out on the water is a healing thing. And in spite of their occasional bitching Toby and Friendly were not bad company.

"We've got three sea trout and two perch," Toby said, checking in the cooler. "That's not bad."

"Maybe we should switch to bloodworms," Friendly

136

suggested, wiping the beer off his upper lip. He crumbled the can with one hand and tossed it into the compound bucket with several other dead soldiers. "We only got three more days before they close rock season."

Toby pushed his rod between his hip and upper arm, leaning across the washboard to get himself another ham and cheese sandwich. "It's a window of rockfish opportunity," he remarked, taking a big bite.

"Used to be you could fish for rock all o' the damned time, anytime. Then they got scarce and the fish cops put a ban on 'em. They just opened up the spring and fall seasons last couple years. What we got here is an overfished, overpolluted estuary." He belched comfortably. What is it about men and boats? You put them on one and they turn into either Popeye or Bligh. It's another example of testosterone poisoning.

"You got a real nice boat here, a real nice boat," Friendly remarked, pulling up his reel, then allowing the tip of his rod to come down again. "Somethin's eatin' my bait, I think."

"Yeah. She's one of the last old wooden-hull workboats. She's what they call a Beddoe's Island broad stern. That big ol' stern is why she's so broad in the beam and has that sharp chine; keeps her keel steady on these shallow waters around the Bay. Old Man Mills built her back in the thirties for my father. You look in the cabin on the rising beam and you can see his initials on the underside—*A.M*, Albanus Mills. The man signed his own work. They built a workboat in those days too, built 'em to last. All I ever have to do is put her up on the railway in March and hull 'er out and paint her."

"Say, Hollis, ain't that your daddy comin' down the channel over there?" Toby asked.

I squinted past the 9A can at the workboat a half mile

137

away. She was moving so fast that her bow rose out of the water like a shark fin, but I would have recognized the shape of that boat anywhere.

"That looks like my father's boat," I agreed absently.

Toby waved to the small dark figure beneath the canopy, but the figure at the wheel never even looked in our direction as he swung around the point toward Shadbush Cove and the harbor, leaving a wake behind him.

"What the hell was that all about?"

"Damned if I know."

The wake hit the boat and we began to rock.

Toby cursed grandstanders everywhere, and Friendly began to tell a story about a cop pal of his who actually lived aboard his boat in Inner Harbor. Slowly, the wake from the other boat spread apart and the waters were calm again.

I barely listened to them before I drifted back into the ebb and flow of the wind and the water. The old caisson light, built when there was still a Swann's Island and not a shallow shoal at the mouth of the Santimoke River, was as familiar to me as my own family. They'd taken the keepers off the Bay lighthouses in the forties and fifties when they'd gone to automation, but I'd grown up hearing tales of my great-uncle Bain's days at Swann's Island, he'd lived here with his wife and two lads for eight years, and whenever they got together my mother and her cousins loved to talk about living in the lighthouse, especially when the storms would whip up and howl around the solitary brick column, and how the ice floes would break up around the caisson, causing her to rock back and forth.

From here Turkey Buzzard Point was only about a mile as the crow flies, but you could bet that Busbee

Clinton's house must have seemed a million light-years away when the river froze solid in the winter and they were isolated from the mainland for a week at a time.

I squinted across the bow at the Clinton homeplace for a second, then looked away again. Although from this distance the old place looked like something you could put under a Christmas tree, it still reminded me of my problems with my family and with Jen. But I wasn't about to allow the whole Ornamental Hermit tangle to spoil a perfectly lovely evening on the water.

And it was a lovely evening too. The water was so clear that you could see the diamonds of moonlight dancing on the waves, and the shore was so close you could sometimes catch the smell of blossoming spring when it blew past you on the breeze. It was a warmish evening, so all I needed was a heavy sweatshirt.

". . . never liked those big ol' Mercury V-8's" Friendly was telling Toby, but I didn't listen with both ears. I was content in my own thoughts, as long as I wasn't nagged by my family concerns and unanswered questions.

I felt a series of sudden sharp tugs at my line and reeled it in. The hooks were empty, stripped of bait. "There's a crab down there," I muttered, as much to myself as to the men.

I shifted myself from where I was sitting on the stern washboard and poked the butt of my rod into the holder Toby had screwed into the wood there just for that purpose.

I wanted a cigarette, but since I knew better than to ask to borrow one from Friendly, I contented myself with poking around in the food cooler for a beer and a sandwich. Salt air can make you peckish. The sandwich I drew was tuna on rye bread, made with an oil, green peppercorn, and vinegar dressing. Toby had sliced paper-thin strips of Vidalia onion for the topping. It was heavenly. Even potato chips would have spoiled it. The fishy bait smell on my hands just added to the tang.

The last of the setting sun was turning into a huge orange ball, dipping below the trees, tingeing the darkening sky with red and pink. The rays cast dancing brilliants across the darkening water. Beneath my feet I could feel the currents pulling the boat against the drag anchor, scraping the rocks and ballast ten feet below.

Every once in a while Toby's Findafish would beep, and we would see the dim shapes moving across the monitor beside the wheel.

"Damn, they're down there," Toby remarked with considerable frustration. "They just ain't biting! Maybe we ought to switch over to bloodworms. Maybe they aren't taken' no peeler crabs toni—"

"Hold everything, hon!" Friendly jumped back tucking his rod under his elbow and rolling up on his line. The tip of his long graphite pole bent nearly double as he began to reel in. "My God," he gasped, with complete reverence, "I think I've got a whale on here!"

Toby jumped for the net, and I instinctively reached under the washboards for the gaff.

"Gimme some room here," Friendly gasped. "This thing weighs a ton!"

"Keep it steady; don't break your pace," Toby advised.

Friendly kept reeling, but he wasn't doing it real fast, even though you could tell he was straining against the weight of whatever was on the other end of the line. I could see the beads of sweat breaking out across his forehead with the effort of putting out so much strength.

"How much line did you lay out?" Toby demanded,

bracing himself against the side, the big old net firmly in his hands.

"Not that much—shit, this thing is deadweight!" Friendly panted, but he kept on reeling and reeling and reeling, not so fast now. That expensive rod was almost horseshoed double with the drag of whatever was down there.

" 'S probably an old tire or something," Toby guessed.

"It's just lying there, not fighting at all." Friendly was panting now.

"Toadfish," I suggested.

"Then it's the biggest . . . goddamnedest . . . toadfish . . . in . . . the . . . Chesapeake . . . Bay!" Friendly grunted, but he kept on reeling it in. I honestly thought that rod would snap.

"What weight have you got?" Toby asked.

"Hundred-pound test." Friendly reeled and reeled. I could see that his knuckles were white and his arms were straining under his beaten-up nylon windbreaker. "I . . . am . . . gonna . . . have . . . to . . . cut . . . it . . . loose," he wheezed at last. "It . . . can . . . have . . . my . . . tackle, but I'm . . . damned . . .if . . . it . . . Will break . . . this . . . *four-hundred-dollar rod!*"

Just at that moment, about twenty feet away, something broke water.

"Hang in there, boy, we got 'er!" Toby crowed. "There she is!"

"But what is it?" I asked, squinting at the huge shape drawing closer and closer to our stern. "It looks like a store dummy!"

"Dummy, hell," Toby hissed.

It was big and pinkish-white, like a hog. For a minute I thought someone was using a slaughtered pig for bait,

141

but then I saw the hand raise up out of the water, as if it were waving at us.

Toby grabbed the gaff and dragged the thing up to the stern, turning it over so that we could see what was left of its bloated face. The teeth were exposed in a grinning rictus. An eel slithered out of its mouth and disappeared into the dark water. As Toby hooked the head up, several large crabs that had been feeding on one ear clung furiously to their meal. A length of thick wire was wrapped around its knees and elbows, trussing it up like a chicken.

Friendly made a hacking sound in the back of his throat.

"Jesus H. Christ," Toby said, "it's Busbee Clinton!"

Remember when I said that there were some things that humankind was not meant to contemplate and that a buck-naked Busbee Clinton was one of them?

Boy, was I ever right on the money.

CHAPTER 13

FLOATER

"WE'RE READY TO ROCK AND ROLL, SERGEANT," THE head fish cop told Friendly.

The Beddoe's Island V.F.D., the state police, and the Department of Natural Resources people were everywhere. On Toby's boat, on their boats. There were divers in the river, helicopters in the air, trucks and cruisers and ambulances on land with lonesome flashing lights that spun crazily out across the river.

Even though nightfall had long since stretched dark fingers across our little corner of the world, they had enough artificial light out there to film a full-length feature. A horrible surrealism hung over the whole scene.

I was never so glad to come back from a fishing trip in my life.

Toby had radioed in for help, and Friendly had told us to leave the corpse where it was, in the water, bobbing along the stern of the boat like Moby Dick. "It's a damned sad world, hon, when a man can't even go fishin' without turnin' up a floater. And a damned small world when two out of three people on board the boat can ID the corpse. It's a cult. Leave 'im overboard, Toby; we don't want to disturb any possible evidence."

"Good thing too," Toby had growled. "I'm not hauling that son of a bitch up here so he can mess up my clean deck! Let 'im stay out there with the eels and the crabs where he belongs!"

It was hard to tell who was more angry, Toby or Friendly. You'd think Busbee had done it on purpose.

It seemed as if we were out there for hours waiting for the search-and-rescue teams to arrive. With nighfall a thin, chill wind began to pick up, and Busbee started to rock on the tide, rhythmically banging into the hull, creating a muffled, hollow echo that reverberated through the whole boat. When I looked at him an oyster crab slithered out of Busbee's mouth and swam away.

That's when I leaned over the side and vomited up my sandwich and two bottles of Dos Equiis. I supposed it would be a while before I could eat crabs again too; Friendly tried to drive them away with the gaff, but they returned again and again, driven into a feeding frenzy by the smell of decomposing in the water. Many of them had been hibernating deep in the mud bottom all winter and were hungry for a good meal.

143

Beautiful swimmer—that's what the blue crab's scientific name means in Latin. Scavengers that feed on things both dead and dying, they didn't look too beautiful to me that night.

"Maybe we should fish him for a while before the fire department comes," Toby suggested, and he and Friendly began to laugh. Real gallows humor for a couple of tough guys.

"I hear they're gettin' one seventy-five for number-one crabs," Friendly chuckled. He and Toby played the searchlight over Busbee. I rinsed my mouth out with melted ice and popped an Altoids because I really needed a cigarette, then stood forward by the helm so I wouldn't have to look at those filmy sockets and that gaping mouth or that white, bloated body.

"How long has he been in the water?" Toby asked conversationally. The two of them stood in the stern, looking over the side at their catch of the day.

"I can't tell, but I hope the medical examiner can. Looks to me like he drowned. Look at the foam comin' out of his nose and his mouth. See how wrinkly the skin on his hands and feet skin is, like a prune? He's been in the water for some hours," Friendly replied in a matter-of-fact voice. "But he's not bloated, so it can't have been so long. We had one guy in Middle River one time, he fell off a Polish freighter in the fall and drifted all winter. By the time we found him he'd turned to soap."

"I dunno." Toby was doubtful. "I saw a guy once, tied an engine block around his waist with baling wire and committed suicide by jumping overboard out to Jack's Hole, down to Cook's Point. It's three hundred feet deep out there. He was all the hell tangled up when he come up. Corpse gas made him bob right up after a week or so in hot weather, engine block and all."

I wished they would shut up, but I didn't have the strength to ask them. Instead, I went below and found Toby's foul-weather gear and wrapped up in the jacket. It smelled of mildew.

From time to time the radio crackled and Toby would speak to someone, giving our location again and again.

Still, it was an hour before we saw the running lights of a Department of Natural Resources Whaler, and by then my teeth were chattering, I was so cold. But not as cold as Busbee Clinton.

"We better throw some bumpers over." Friendly sighed. "He's banging against the boat, and it will damage the corpse."

"Corpse, hell. That sucker better not put a hurting on my boat," Toby snapped nervously.

The high distant roar of approaching boats signaled that our nightmare was just starting.

After a search that lasted for more endless hours, all they found was Busbee Clinton. No overturned boat, no other corpses, just a naked dead guy. Thank God Friendly took charge; Toby, whose tolerance for rules of order is thin, was close to exploding after the third time someone in a uniform asked us all the same questions again.

"If I'd known it was gonna be all this trouble," Toby grumbled, "I woulda cut that son of a bitch loose and let the crabs finish what they started." Since my cousin has an atavistic dislike for law enforcement—save for his inexplicable male-bonding thing with Friendly—I wasn't surprised.

"If I'd been thinking, instead of hoping I'd hooked a stray shark or a skate or something good, I would have cut him loose too," Friendly muttered unhappily.

145

By the time they'd hauled Busbee out of the water, brought him back to Shadbush Cove, zipped him into a plastic bag, and waited for Doc Westmore to pronounce, everyone put their heads together and concluded there was foul play involved. They all nodded wisely, like this was some great discovery. It must have been a slow night.

After a long time and a lot of bad jokes, the musical tinkle of pockets full of miniature liquor bottles announced the arrival of our county medical examiner, the only and one Doc Westmore.

They steered Doc away from live patients years before, but he still earns his minimum daily requirement of Stoly by pronouncing corpses dead enough to send up the medical examiner's office in Baltimore, where they can do the real work.

Doc—fragile, elderly, and pickled in enough vodka to outlast a frozen woolly mammoth—tripped forward. "This better be good, gettin' me away from *Diagnosis: Murder,*" he grumbled.

Someone unzipped the body bag and he peered over his wire-rimmed glasses at the contents. With the toe of one elegant wing-tip brogan, he hauled off and kicked at the corpse as hard as he could.

"What'd you go and do that for, Doc?" one of the paramedics asked lazily.

Doc's glasses glittered in the searchlights. From a pocket of his duck-embroidered sport jacket, he withdrew one of his tiny bottles and took a healthy swig.

"That's Busbee Clinton," he observed matter-of-factly. "I just wanted to make sure that the common sorry son of a bitch was really dead."

Everyone nodded.

146

"And he is," Doc chuckled, "and there must be a God, because he is! Low-down bastard! Haul his sorry ass out of here, boys; he'll be warming up a chair in hell tonight." He had another swig to celebrate as they led him away, the sound of his jingling bottles fading into the night.

"Everyone seems to have loved the deceased," Friendly muttered.

"Hell," Jim Bob LaMonte, the search-and-rescue chief, observed, "Busbee Clinton's own mother probably hated him. If this turns out to be a homicide— and it sure looks like one to me—you wouldn't be able to get a fair jury in this county. They'd end up votin' a medal to the killer."

Friendly didn't say anything, but I could tell he wasn't too thrilled.

While Toby cleaned up the boat I took his keys and went back to his place to try to get warm and cleaned up. Peaches Brennan, the island's serial divorcee, who pinch-hits for Toby, had long since shut the bar up and gone home; it was hours past last call.

I figured fire and rescue people would be coming in, so I set up the coffeemaker (caf and decaf) and popped myself a diet Pepsi, looking longingly at the cigarette machine in the corner. Although Toby's always looks as if it's 4:00 A.M. on some dark night of the soul, when it really was 4:00 A.M. on some dark night of the soul it looked perfectly normal, all dim and illuminated by neon beer signs and the trashy flash of the jukebox. I turned the heat up and threw myself into a booth over by the pool table, where I could lie down on a flat surface and close my eyes.

I was tired to the bone.

I must have fallen asleep, or into that state between

awake and asleep where everything flows over your consciousness like a tide. I was dimly aware of people talking in low voices over by the bar.

"Why can't Hollis see me? What happened to Busbee? Is he dead?"

"Hush, Renata, it's all right. Busbee's dead now. He can't hurt anyone else, not ever again."

Just a dream, but I thought Sam was in it, and maybe Renata Ringwood Clinton, shapes moving around the bar, gray shadows, speaking in whispers like blowing ashes.

"Some of us she can see, others of us she can't. Let me handle this, Renata . . . ."

And then someone was shaking me awake. I opened my eyes to look into Ormand Friendly's face. He looked like hell. His chin was dark with stubble and there were deep puffy pouches under his eyes. Behind him I was aware of exhausted people shuffling around in their rubber boots, of the door swinging open and closed, dawn falling into the dim sanctuary of Toby's Bar and Grill. The smell of coffee, tobacco smoke, and frying bacon hung in the thick air.

"Are you awake, hon?" Friendly asked me.

"Sort of." I sat up. My back felt as if tiny Japanese samurai had been sticking swords into it all night, or as if I had fallen asleep on a Naugahyde booth bench at a hell bar. "What's happening?"

"Well, we've decided that we're gonna treat this as a homicide," he said. "Of course, we still have to get the ME's office to pronounce, but it seems pretty obvious that this Clinton guy was tied up and dumped overboard to drown. I've been talking to a lot of people from the fire department down here who knew Clinton."

"Okay," I said, yawning. "I can work with that."

148

"Hollis, I am deeply and truly sorry," Friendly said slowly, "but you know I have to question Perk about this."

I didn't like the way he was saying that. It woke me up though.

Oh yeah, now I was wide awake.

I wasn't about to waste my time wondering why he wanted to talk to Perk. Everyone on the island knew how Dad felt about Busbee, and the bad blood there had been between them for years. The crab strike was just the latest symptom.

Remembering how we had seen Dad's boat going into the harbor like a maritime bat out of Bay hell, I knew he had a couple of good reasons to want to talk to my father.

Still, it made me feel sick, sicker than I felt seeing Busbee all covered up with feasting crabs.

"If you question Dad," I said, my voice unsteady, you'll have to question everyone else on the island too. He wasn't the only one who hated Busbee, you know! Maybe you ought to talk to Jennifer Clinton, and H. P. Wescott, and Billy Chinaberry too!"

I was amazed at the ease with which I could and would rat out some other likely suspects. I dislike snitches and was ashamed to discover the ease with which I named names.

Family is family, and I knew my father wouldn't kill anyone.

Busbee Clinton was the only person I'd ever seen him lose his temper over. I felt even sicker as I remembered the scene in the yard on Sunday night. There must have been fifteen or twenty people there who had heard Dad threaten to kill Busbee. And a couple of them, like Mertis, were constitutionally incapable of keeping quiet about it, police or no police. Sooner or later Friendly would hear about that. But I was damned if he would hear about it from me.

Friendly just looked at me. "I'm going over there now," he said slowly, watching me as if he was afraid I would hit him. "I'm going to talk to Perk and to Ms. Clinton."

"I'll come with you," I said, but Friendly's hand on my shoulder pushed me down.

"No, you go home and get some sleep. There's nothing you can do here now."

While I was still trying to find a good reason why I should go to my folks' house with him, Friendly disappeared.

Toby put a mug of coffee in front of me. "Don't worry," he said. "I called over to Uncle Perk and Aunt Doll's and warned 'em that Orm was comin'," he said. Then he waited, and I could tell just by looking at him that there was bad news to follow.

"What did Dad say? Do they want me to come over there?" I asked.

Toby shook his head. "You know what Perk and Doll can be like," he said.

"I'm still in the doghouse, huh?"

Toby nodded. "Your dad said for you to stay out of this, that he'll handle it. I wouldn't go around there today." He shrugged and walked away.

I sat up, yawning. The rescuers were hunched around the bar, where Toby and Peaches Brennan were dishing out bacon and eggs and hot coffee to fatigued men and women who could barely lift a utensil to their mouths. There was pure exhaustion in the defeated curve of their spines. They drooped over their plates, almost too tired to talk in complete sentences.

On an island that depends upon the water for economic survival, drownings are not uncommon. And yet we never get used to them either; each one is a tragedy, even if the floater is a man as universally hated as Busbee Clinton.

Still, there are limits.

"I said, I says, look, I am not putting no dead body in my clean ambulance. If we transport a corpse, especially if we have to take it all the way to Baltimore, we have to disinfect the whole thing. Do you know how much work that is, disinfecting an entire ambulance? Look, I'd do it if it were one of the boys, one of the watermen gone overboard, but Busbee Clinton? Shee-yut. Let 'at sumbitch stay out there, that's all."

"They called Parsons Dreedle over to the funeral parlor, and he come with the meat wagon. He'll take ole Busbee up to Bal'mur."

"And he won't have to disinfect a whole ambulance over it either. Hunh! You ever disinfect an entire ambulance? It's a job of work!"

"Too much like work, if you ast me."

"Not for a prick like Busbee Clinton. He was one evil bastard."

"I heard they're gonna take the daughter down there to Dreedle's to identify the body. She's some big-time actress on the stories. It was Busbee, all right, I got a good look at 'im. Somebody wrapped 'im up with wire and tossed 'im overboard, that's what I think. Poor woman, to have that happen to her."

"I heard that *Hapless Hearts* girl was on the island, the one that was so mean to that Stud guy when he had her up in that cabin . . ."

I put my head down on the table.

"You know, Perk is a prime suspect. As soon as your

151

cop pal has enough evidence, he'll arrest your dad, that's the word on the street. Everyone's still talking about the big fight he and Busbee had Sunday night—"

I saw Sam's dim shape sitting opposite me in the booth. He was reclining against the wall, one arm lying along the back of the seat, the other one on the table. He tilted his head slightly, watching me. I couldn't read his expression; his face was in shadow.

"Dad couldn't have killed Busbee. That's not his style," I whispered, with one eye on the bar. But no one else could hear me above the sound of Toby's turning on the morning news. Busbee's drowning merited fifteen seconds of confused talking-head verbiage from a moussed-up blond anchorwoman. ". . . daughter is daytime-drama-actress Jennifer Clinton—"

"Shit," I said succinctly.

Sam just looked at me as if I were a hopeless case, which maybe I was. "I think we need to talk to the Old Man and Billy Chinaberry. Get to the bottom of this Ornamental Hermit business. That's where we'll find out who killed the lovely and talented Busbee Clinton!"

"What you mean, we, white man?" I rubbed my eyes. My head was beginning to pound. I thought for a minute, running the whole back story through my mind. "I just can't believe that my father could kill anyone, unless you count that hunting accident in the blind that time."

Sam shrugged. "I could bet that lots of other people could and do believe he did it, just because he's from Beddoe's Island, where you could expect that kind of behavior from people."

Sometimes Sam talks just to hear himself, but I knew there was some truth in what he was saying now.

I took a deep breath. "So far I've tried to avoid this

whole stupid mess like it was a plague of editors. I really don't care what the goddamned Ornamental Hermit is, or whether or not Jen Clinton thinks someone killed her mother and dumped her car off a bridge thirty years ago. For all I give a flying fart in hell, H. P. Wescott and Billy Chinaberry can jump out the creek. But," I sputtered, "when you start draggin' my family into it, you've got me to deal with!"

"The game is afoot, Hollis! We've got a mystery to solve! This time," Sam added thoughtfully, "it's a mission of mercy."

"This time, it's personal!" I snarled.

CHAPTER 14

THE UNUSUAL SUSPECTS

I THINK THERE MUST BE A PAGE I'VE MISSED IN THE AP Stylebook that says every paper with a circulation under twenty thousand *must* have some retired geezer writing a column of good ol' boy bonhomie, outdoorsy ramblings, rose-tinted nostalgia and garbled half-truths that just skirt libel.

I'll bet your local paper has one; I know ours does.

B. R. "Bunky" Bozman, president emeritus of the Santimoke Bank and Trust, was writing so many letters to the editor that Rig finally decided to pay him a pittance to write a weekly column, thereby eliminating the need to shell out the slightly larger pittance required to keep the syndicated pontifications of George Will and Ellen Goodman appearing on the *Gazette*'s editorial page. Squeezing another two hundred dollars a year out of the paper for the Owner got him a thousand-dollar raise, we heard down in the trenches.

I think Bunky's wife Lorraine was secretly paying Rig; Bunky's new status as a columnist kept him out and about rather than underfoot at home, where he had evidently been using his leisure time to tell her how to do the housework she had been accomplishing perfectly well on her own for the past forty-three years. But that's just what I think, and I can't prove it.

What I could prove was that the author of the weekly musing found in "The Rain Won't Hurt the Rhubarb" could be found every Saturday morning taking a Bloody Mary brunch at the Santimoke Yacht Club, founded by his great-great-grandfather. Where my chances of getting in the door unannounced and uninvited were about the same as a snowball's in the Southwestern corner of hell.

For some strange reason Bunky and I actually *like* each other, so when I called early that morning and asked him to escort me and another person to our local bastion of propertied, private Protestant privilege, he didn't even ask why.

"Come on down, gal," he chuckled. "I'll buy you all a drink or seventeen, honey. Us reporters gotta stick together, ya know. Are we hot on the Busbee Clinton murder?"

"You figured me out, Bunky," I said as I hung up the phone.

Sam, sitting in the rocking chair in my bedroom, the sunlight of yet another day pouring through his translucent body, leaned back in the chair and crossed his hands behind his head.

"That's where the Old Man can be found every Saturday morning, in the men's bar," he grinned.

"You've got to hand it to him for belonging to one of

the most segregated clubs on the Eastern Shore," I said, rifling through my closet for something shabby enough to allow me to pass unnoticed among the Moldy Old Money. "Not only do they exclude anyone who's not a pure white Episcopalian who's family's been here since the birth of Christ—with a dollar for each year—but they separate the sexes. Who ever heard of a men's bar and a ladies' lounge?"

I pulled out a khaki skirt and ransacked the back of my drawers until I found a white turtleneck and a navy blue cable-knit sweater. Thank God for Mom's rummage sales; I could disguise myself as anything in society's stereotypes—from a respectable working woman to a Middle Eastern terrorist—on a moment's notice. "I draw the line at knee socks," I told Sam. But I had the navy flats.

"At least you won't embarrass Bunky," he said.

"Nothing embarrasses Bunky. This is a man who slapped a First Lady on the ass and called her a real baby doll—at an inaugural ball," I replied thickly, struggling to close the waistband of a skirt I hadn't worn in a decade. "I might be banned forever from stately Wescott Manor, but I'm damned if the Old Man'll elude me on public ground."

Sam chuckled. "Well, you wouldn't have been banned from the old homeplace if you hadn't figured out all about the family's wetland developing that just happened to be ever so slightly illegal. That mess cost the family millions to clean up, you know."

"There's millions more where that came from," I snapped. The turtleneck was choking me. "And I'm betting that H.P. knows more about the Ornamental Hermit than he's letting on."

"*Cherchez l'hermite,*" Sam intoned. "At least Ed Poe

gave you something to work with, didn't he?"

"He just put out more puzzle pieces. What does a living garden gnome have to do with Busbee?"

"And with Renata? Don't forget that. It seems that all this stuff has been happening since they found her body," Sam pointed out. "Whatever's going on, it seems to me that it has a lot to do with Renata surfacing after all these years."

I ran my hairbrush through the unruly mess on top of my head and tied it back with an Hermès scarf.

"I just don't like the idea that Jen's down there with my parents. There's something wrong with her tales of the invisible stalker. There's something wrong with her whole story." I turned from the mirror and looked at Sam. "What was Dad doing out there on the water at that time of the evening, anyway? He's not crabbing, and even if he were, he would have been in long before that, wouldn't he?"

Sam inclined his head. "I'm a ghost, not Dr. Laura," he pointed out. "She may think she's omniscient; I know my limits."

"Friendly's a cop," I fumed, stepping into the bathroom to do my eyes. "He thinks like a cop. The most likely suspect is the easiest one to go after. Even if he recuses himself from the case for conflict of interest, the guy they bring in from the next barracks is gonna think the same thing."

"Only more so," Sam said. He rocked back and forth in the chair, pleased with his ability to make simple material objects move around.

"These guys have no creativity whatsoever," I fumed.

"Unlike us. We are very creative."

"We know a bad deal when we see it," I agreed, smudging a little lipstick on. "When they get the ME's

156

report back from Baltimore, they'll charge Dad."

"Your mother will have a heart attack."

"Maybe literally," I said, thinking about that herring roe. "If Dad doesn't have one first. You think I should call down to the folks?"

Sam shook his head. "By now they probably blame you. You know how your folks can get all excited about something and go off half-cocked, like they did Monday when you brought Jennifer Clinton over and then didn't believe her stalker story. Why call up and get a raft from them?"

"They always wished I was more of a little lady like Jen." A form of sibling rivalry had reared its ugly head. "The key is the Ornamental Hermit, and H.P. knows what it is!"

"Atta girl!" Sam cheered. "We'll get him!"

I dropped my lipstick. "What do you mean, 'we'?" I asked him.

Sam gave me a look of such innocence that I knew he had something in mind. I poked my head out of the bathroom. "Now, look, you—" But he had disappeared. The rocker moved gently back and forth a time or two, then stopped. An absolute calm settled on the house that I didn't like one bit.

Bunky—seventyish, mischievous, and stooped—couldn't have been more excited if I'd told him we had just won the club regatta. "I'm finally a part of an investigative report," he chuckled when I met him in the yacht-club parking lot. "Stop the presses," he called, when we were joined by Santimoke County's State's Attorney, Ms. Athena "Hardass" Hardcastle. Totally soigné in her fair isle sweater and wraparound skirt. She had found a pair of knee socks and a light-ship basket.

157

Perfect.

The look Bunky gave Athena was pure admiration; she *is* a gorgeous woman. "Yes, my dear ladies, stop the presses!"

We were going to stop the presses, all right.

As we entered the mahogany-paneled members' dining room, the smell of mildew and old people hit me like a slap. It was like walking into the student union at college; everyone turned around to stare as if we had just dropped in from another planet, which maybe we had.

Bunky, with the confidence of one who is so old family and old money and so establishment they just don't give a damn, offered each of us an arm and allowed an uncomfortable waiter to lead us across the room to an empty table. And it was a long, long room, packed to the paneling with happy brunchers getting a good start on the day's ethyl infusion.

Elbows bent to raise glasses to withered lips froze, laughter and conversation fled, and eyebrows were raised to places where hairlines used to be. The collective intake of breath was audible.

"Your usual, Sir?" the geriatric servitor asked, cutting us girls with a fishy eye.

"Thank you, John. And the ladies will have . . ."

"Mimosa for me," I said.

Athena smiled, waving at a lawyer or two across the room. "I think I shall have a very Bloody Mary," she said sweetly. She leveled that smile at Bunky. "So," she drawled, "this is what you white folk do in your spare time, hmm?"

Did I mention that Athena is African-American?

A stunningly beautiful woman, with skin the color of polished mahogany and a regal elegance that made

158

every other woman in the room look like an mutation. It doesn't hurt that she has a law degree from Princeton and the sort of sangfroid that makes her enjoy little escapades like this, especially in a good cause like making her case on a homicide.

Bunky may be a 3R, but he's a cool 3R. I could see that he was going to enjoy writing a column about this little episode. If Sam had lived to make old bones, I think he would have become a Bunky. You could see that in spite of the differences you'd think would divide them, he and Athena were each other's new best friend.

"We old Princeton alums have to stick together," he was telling her, oblivious to the shocked stares all around them. "You know, Ms. Hardcastle, they make a wonderful crab omelet here."

"That sounds wonderful! You know, I can't believe Dr. Yacky was teaching when you were there too. He *must* be a hundred!"

While the two of them had old home week, I pretended to stare at the faded black-and-white photographs of sailboats on the wall, but I was really scanning the room for a certain familiar face. On the whole I thought the three of us were doing a pretty good job of ignoring the shocked stares of the bigots all around us.

The great thing was, they couldn't throw Bunky out. The same rules that excluded Athena from membership here also stated clearly that the same membership descended, as irrevocable as a gene, through the Founding Commodores' descendants. If Bunky decided to pick up his marbles and go home, the Santimoke Yacht Club would be up for sale as waterfront condo development. Bunky doesn't give a damn.

No one even noticed when I slipped away from the

table and went in search of big game. They were all too busy staring at the first African-American woman in their midst who wasn't there to wash the floors or scrub the toilets or cook the crab cakes.

H. P. Wescott was at his table in the corner, under the pictures of dead commodores. I didn't know the people at his table, but I guessed that they were Hiromoto Industries and that he was anxious to impress them by bringing them here. Like everyone else, they were staring blankly at Athena and Bunky.

"Come with me and no one gets hurt," I whispered in his ear. "Otherwise, I'll make a bigger scene than this one."

The Old Man jerked back into the present as if I'd hit him with a cattle prod. He turned cold eyes on me. They were Sam's eyes, without the warmth or the humor. He opened his mouth to say something, but I guess he wasn't fooled by the bland look he saw on my face. He tossed his starched linen napkin on the table and stood up, towering over me.

I led him into the sacred precincts of the men's bar.

It was deserted at this time of day; the really good down-and-dirty drinking doesn't start until after brunch. An elderly bartender was leaning on the counter, watching a basketball game on ESPN. When he saw us he decided he had pressing business in the kitchen.

"I've always wondered what the charm of this place was," I said, looking around at the decor, which was down-at-heel deco horseshoe-bar teak, with a nautical motif of hawsers, running lights, and portholes.

"Get to the point, Hollis," the Old Man growled, drumming his thick fingers on the bar top. "What do you want now?"

God, he was really mad.

160

I saw Sam appear on the other side of the bar, leaning forward as he gazed intently at his father.

Even if H.P. could see ghosts—which he couldn't—that thousand-mile stare should have made the hair on the back of his neck stand up. All that unfinished father and son business was packed into one long look.

Unconsciously, H.P.'s hand went up and he rubbed his neck with an uneasy hand. But his eyes never left mine, even as his face flushed a deep aubergine.

"You think you're clever, don't you?"

"I was taught by experts." I honored my former father-in-law with what I hoped was a bland smile. "You're a hard man to get a hold of. Your secretary says you're in a perpetual meeting, and I couldn't get past the front door at stately Mandrake Manor if I tried." I dropped my smile. "We pulled Busbee Clinton out of the river last night."

Evidently, he hadn't heard the news that morning. The flush drained from his face, leaving his skin the color of dirty ice. He sat down heavily on a barstool, grunting.

"Reach over there behind the bar and get me that bottle of Wild Turkey and a shot glass," he commanded me, and I did as I was told. When the Old Man says jump, it's natural to say "How high?"

"How?" he asked as he poured himself a shot and downed it in one gulp. His hand was shaking.

"I don't know. My cousin Toby, Detective Sergeant Ormand Friendly, and I went fishing last night out by the Swann's Island light. Friendly thought he had hooked a whale, but it turned out to be Busbee, trussed up with wire. I saw him myself. I knew who it was."

The Old Man swore. Now, the Old Man had a world-class vocabulary of obscenities, blasphemies, and

161

condemnations, and he was at his most creative when employing them. Even I, who have been around watermen all my life, had to admire the way he could cuss.

The very air turned blue with the color, selection, and content of his speech, which started out by condemning Busbee, his ancestry, his person, his soul, and his corpse to a life of eternal burning hell. Then he moved on to Beddoe's Island, Santimoke County, Maryland, and the world beyond before moving into capitalism and the evil chicanery of those with whom one was forced to do business. He finished up with a crescendo that graphically castigated the vagaries of universal fate and then his poor luck in specific.

When he finished he poured himself another shot.

Sam grinned. "That's my dad," he said proudly. "Got a mouth on him like a French whore."

I poured myself a shot after that.

"You would think that miserable toad would have enough sense to keep out of harm's way," H.P. fumed. "Just like him to get himself killed."

"You make it sound as if he did it to inconvenience you."

The Old Man cut me a look. "Well, it is a damned inconvenience. I'd just signed a contract with him to buy that miserable place of his. I had in mind putting in some condos down there." He shook his head. "And yes, I have all the permits in place, and no, it's not some blithering damned bleeding-heart wetland! Perfectly buildable property, Turkey Buzzard Point. Now I guess I'll have to deal with the daughter, but I hate the idea of keeping the contractors on retainer for another damned six months waiting for probate."

Sam snickered. "Ask him about the last time he did

162

business with Busbee," he suggested.

"I'm getting to that," I snapped before I thought.

"Getting to what?" H.P. asked. "I can't see that the girl, that soap actress, would want that mess down there. Cleaning that place up would cost more than it's worth in the inheritance tax alone. Damn, I'd like to dig that son of a bitch up so I could kill him all over again!"

"I would think that you would be reluctant to get into another business deal with him after that whole thing with the Bayside Hotel," I offered.

"Hit the hot button," Sam encouraged me.

Evidently, it was a very hot button indeed. The Old Man all but had steam coming out of his ears. "The Bayside! The goddamned Bayside! What that cost us first and last! And Billy and I only went into it because we . . . we owed him a favor from the war."

I caught the slight hesitation in his voice. "A favor from the war? Is that what you call it?" I asked.

"What do you know about that?" H.P. demanded.

"What's the Ornamental Hermit?" I counter-attacked.

He clenched a fist and brought it down on the bar. From the way he was looking at me I felt he might have wanted to bring it down on my head. "What the hell do you want to know about that for?" His face was so close to mine I could see the gin blossoms in his cheeks and nose.

Sam said something, but I didn't catch it. "Because right now it looks as if my father is the prime suspect," I hissed. "And I'm not going to stand by and let them pin this on him so a rich man can walk free."

H.P. was breathing heavily. For a big man he could move awfully fast when he wanted to, and he had a temper. So when he stood up I got ready to move fast.

"You think *I* killed Busbee Clinton?" he asked me in

163

a truly awful tone.

"You've done it now!" Sam exclaimed.

"Somebody did!" I was raising my voice now.

H.P. opened his mouth. To my utter astonishment he threw back his head and laughed. Great, bellowing peals of laughter. He laughed until the tears literally ran down his cheeks, his massive body shaking all over. "I killed Busbee. Oh, that is rich! That's so good!" He shook his head. "I killed Busbee Clinton! I should have killed that son of a bitch fifty years ago when I had the chance, but no, I didn't kill him."

From the pocket of his navy blue blazer he pulled out a handkerchief and dabbed at his eyes. "Hollis, you are a funny creature! I never killed Busbee Clinton!"

The more he laughed, the madder I became. "This isn't a joke, H.P.! Not when my father's the prime suspect!"

His laughter gradually faded, and he shook his head. "No, it's no joke," he agreed. "No joke at all. Although from what I hear, there was plenty of bad blood there. But if all the people who wanted to kill Busbee at any given time were laid end to end, the line would stretch from here to China. Not that I would have minded killing him; it's just that I wouldn't do it now, when I was about to finally recoup some of the money he lost me in that Bayside Hotel fiasco." He lowered his head and looked at me from beneath his bushy eyebrows. "So, you want to know about the Ornamental Hermit, huh?" he asked sullenly.

"I think there's some connection between Renata being found and Busbee being killed," I admitted. "I think whoever killed Busbee knows something about what really happened to Renata all those years ago."

H.P. snorted. "I've already got buyers lined up for

those condos," he said. "Anyway, the police haven't even built a case yet. By the time they start asking questions they'll have enough suspects to start a new county. Perk'll be just fine, you wait and see. It'll turn out to be suicide or a robbery or something. I never knew a man who could cut his own nose off to spite his face the way Busbee could. When he was rolling in high cotton he sure enough found a way to burn down the field ever' damned time."

"What is the connection between Renata and the Ornamental Hermit. H.P.? Tell me that much."

Did I see the smallest spark of anxiety in those cold blue eyes?

"Go talk to Billy Chinaberry," he said, straightening his tie. "I've said all I'm gonna say without talking to my lawyer—"

"I think he means it," Sam said just before he disappeared.

Dysfunctional family reunion everyone brings a covered dish and an unresolved issue. Hollis is right about that.

I may have disappeared from mortal view, but I was still watching my father after Hollis left the building. Death doesn't change some things, like the way I felt about the Old Man. I had to admire his grudging respect for Hollis, for one thing. It takes a tough person to understand another tough person, and for all that he fussed and fumed about her, he also understood that she wasn't going to let go of this story, no matter what.

I watched as he poured himself another shot, nursing it as he stared out the window at the sticks of the sailboats parked at the docks. I sensed something a lot like fear.

I wished that Hollis could see and hear Renata; that would have made everything so much easier. But there are some time-space coordinates that even I can't use to bend the Rules. The living have to work some things out on their own. Besides, what good would it do?

Was it a blank for the Old Man?

A terrible thought came into my mind.

"Father," I asked, even though I knew he couldn't hear me. "Old Man, what have *you done this time?"*

CHAPTER 15

DEAD MAN SQUAWKING REDUX

"WESCOTT TOLD ME YOU WERE COMING." Chinaberry, in butcher's apron and gloves, examined a pot containing a blooming tulip. To my untrained eye it looked like a deep purple rather than an inky black. All around us the army of pots, carried outside in a wheeled cart, were filled with tulips just about to bloom.

Was the Ornamental Hermit somewhere in this garden?

True spring had come to Water Garden in the first pink blush of warm weather. The weeping cherry and the flowering peaches splashed against the glass windows, and the landscape was filled with blues, purples, reds, and pinks as a small army of gardeners transplanted the tulips from pots to well-mulched, rigidly symmetrical beds.

"The philosophy of the formal garden is the imposition of order and regulation on nature, wild and unfettered," Chinaberry remarked conversationally. "It's an especial Age of Reason conceit."

Imposition of order was certainly going on all around me as I followed the housekeeper's directions to "the formal beds," as she had called the precise geometric gardens that surrounded the fountain. Water splashed from the mouth of the rooster and was caught in the deep scalloped bowl. As we walked past it, it sprayed us with a few stray droplets.

Chinaberry selected another blooming tulip from a cart and examined it closely before handing it to one of the groundspeople, who used it to fill in a well-mulched bed whose grids went from pure white through yellow to red, then purple, then black flowers. I felt like Alice in Wonderland.

"I was somewhat sorry to hear Busbee was dead—but not entirely surprised." He smiled wearily, and I noted again the waxy pallor of his skin and the deep purple blotches under his eyes.

"Come take a look at this," he said, gesturing me to come closer to another tulip he was examining. "You can see that it's quite dark, but there's a white calyx. Interesting. I find genetics quite interesting."

"Yes, I recall you said that breeding tulips was one of the things you wanted in your obituary," I said as we strolled toward the boxwood maze. The week's warm weather had filled it with tiny yellow-green shoots of new life.

"We can talk alone in here," he said. "Away from interested ears."

Once again I allowed the high green walls to swallow me up as I followed him on the meandering trail that led to the heart of the labyrinth. I hoped that I would arrive at the heart of the puzzle once we were in there.

"Ah, yes, you wrote my obituary, I recall now. It won't be long before you'll be printing it." Sighing,

Chinaberry settled down on the bench beside me, pushing his hands into the pockets of his jacket. He sighed wearily. "That tuckered me. Fifty years ago I would have run that distance and called you in from this center."

"Fifty years ago I wasn't even born," I replied thoughtfully. The presence of death made me feel philosophical and sad. It was clear that Chinaberry was a man on a budget of time.

"I feel sorry for you kids," he said. "Ours was the last good war. I've done some things I'm not proud of, but I was proud of what I did in the war—most of it." He sucked in his breath. "Wescott, Clinton, and I fought in the Battle of the Bulge, you know. We came through a lot together, fightin' the Germans." He snorted. "Now my company sells 'em Poultry Packers."

"Is that where the Ornamental Hermit came from? Looted Nazi art?" I asked.

Chinaberry shook his head. "I'm getting to that. Give me a chance." He began to cough, a deep, gasping hack that came from deep in his lungs and made him reach for breath. It was a while before he recovered.

We sat in silence for a moment. A robin perched on the hedge and stared at us, its head cocked to one side. Then it flew away.

"We all met up in Paris." He no longer saw me, but looked instead into a past that had been gone for fifty years. "As you can imagine, Busbee working as a quartermaster was like setting the fox to guard the henhouse. He had become a one-man black market! Anything you wanted, you could get it from Busbee—at a price. Chocolate, cigarettes, nylon stockings, T-bone steaks, women, boys, cocaine—it was incredible. Busbee was a born hustler. He made money. Lots of money."

"The foundation of all his fortunes," I offered dryly.

Chinaberry removed a medical inhaler from his pocket and put it to his lips. It seemed to ease his breathing. "Busbee's great talent," he continued, "was knowing everyone else's price. He had a visceral instinct for knowing exactly what you wanted, sometimes before you did. And he knew what price you were willing to pay for it. He knew who to connect you with." He wheezed. I waited.

I settled back to listen.

"I came back from the war and took over my dad's chicken houses. Sort o' lost touch with the boys after that. Then one time I was up in Watertown on business. I was in all right by then, had my first processing plant up and running and I was shippin' chickens all over the peninsula and southeastern Pennsylvania. Busbee must have found out that I was in town. One night he and Wescott showed up at my door with a great chance."

An osprey sailed overhead, calling its shrill cry. In the afternoon sun its white and black underside was stained bloodred by some trick of the light.

"They were building a hotel up on Beddoe's Island. This was in the days when folks from Baltimore and Washington came over here during the summer to escape the heat and humidity of the city; they'd just built the Bay Bridge, and everyone who could came to the Shore on vacation and stayed in these resorts, like Tolchester Beach and Claiborne. They figured that a fancy place on the island could be a gold mine."

A piece of the puzzle slid into place. I felt neither elated nor triumphant. There were still too many missing pieces of the puzzle.

"In those days H.P. wasn't the rich man he is today,

169

and neither was I. The Wescott family was on its uppers after the Depression. But he sensed that Clinton was on to something good. Wescott and Clinton have always known the price of everything and the value of nothing," Chinaberry sighed. "When he ran into Busbee somewhere along the line, he figured that Clinton, whose family owned the land, and he, who had the builders, could put up the hotel. But they didn't have all the money they needed, so they offered me a partnership."

He paused again, spreading his long thin fingers out on the thighs of his trousers. "Now, you have to understand that the Eisenhower years were a boom. After the war people bought cars, got married, had some money to spend. A big hotel seemed like a good idea. I had some money, so I came aboard on the Bayside."

"I could understand that." I laughed. "I'm sure Busbee made it seem like a good investment."

He took a deep breath. "Like I said, Busbee knew everyone's price. He knew that Wescott was making some money building houses, and he knew that I was doin' okay with the chickens. People weren't keeping a few chickens in the backyard in the new suburbs. They wanted to buy them ready from the supermarkets. Busbee always had a hustle. In the war he was the man to see if you wanted nylons or chocolate or cigarettes or a case of C rations and you didn't want to ask too many questions about where these things came from. He'd had some luck, like I had, with the seafood plant. But there was never enough for him. He always had to have more, and he didn't care how he got it."

"Then why did you and H.P. go in on the Bayside Hotel with him?"

Chinaberry flinched. "Renata," he whispered.

"Renata was his ticket." He looked at me. "Why do women always seem to fall in love with the worst possible men? Of course, I'd seen Busbee when he was young and thin and full of dangerous charm. Why she threw herself away on him, I'll never know." He smiled, remembering. "Renata—she was someone special. Beautiful, just beautiful. The Bayside was Renata's idea, and it would have worked, too, if Busbee hadn't started to drink up all the profits. And when he was drunk he was ugly. He drove away customers too. But the nail in our coffin was Ocean City and the beach resorts. By the middle of the sixties, people started going to Ocean City for their vacations." The chicken magnate snorted in disgust. "After a decade the hotel was starting to lose money. If it hadn't been for Renata keeping the books, I would have suspected that Busbee was stealing, but it was going downhill. Finally, Wescott and I realized we had to pull out of it. That's about the time it burned down. Busbee . . . burned down the hotel . . . for insurance . . . sure of that . . . can't prove it . . . any more than . . . Renata could . . ."

Billy Chinaberry began to cough. Deep, racking coughs that sounded as if he were bringing up a lung. From an interior pocket he withdrew a handkerchief, and he hacked into it. I saw that it was stained with blood.

"Here you are, Mr. Chinaberry!" The housekeeper suddenly appeared in the center of the maze, shooting an angry look at me. "You shouldn't be outside without your oxygen on this cool spring night!" She draped a plaid cotton blanket around his shoulders and gently raised him to his feet, as he continued to cough. "That's enough," she told me briskly. "You're upsetting him. He's very ill, you know. You'll have to leave now."

171

I stood up, alarmed and embarrassed.

The housekeeper, who was not a large woman, almost picked the old chicken-magnate man up, guiding him gently back through the maze. It was only then that I noted how thin he was beneath the layers of clothing. I followed, with Chinaberry's coughing hanging in the air.

It was a long trip, made more harrowing by his struggle for air, by the idea that he might fall down in there. But he made it, leaning heavily on the housekeeper, gasping for every breath.

When they emerged, the housekeeper clucked her tongue, wrapping the blanket tightly around him, "Now, Mr. Chinabery, you know that the doctor told you not to get yourself upset!" she scolded him.

"I'm . . . all . . . right . . ." he choked out as he allowed her to lead him toward the house.

Sad and embarrassed, I turned to thread my way through the formal gardens.

"Ms. Ball!" Chinaberry's voice quavered.

I turned.

He hacked, the housekeeper supporting him as he heaved with spasms. "Busbee Clinton . . . killed . . . Renata," he said between gasps. "I . . . know . . . that . . . in . . . my . . . heart!" He began to cough again, almost doubling with the effort.

"What's the Ornamental Hermit?" I called.

The chicken magnate slowly walked back toward that empty house, supported by paid help, and did not look back.

I was no closer to the answer than I had been when I started.

"She's close, Sam, she's close to the truth!" Renata

said to me. We stood, invisible among the hopeful buds of the spring garden, watching the human drama, but unseen ourselves, no more than the lengthening shadows of afternoon in the vast geometric plantation.

"Yeah, but if she's close," I said, "who else also knows? Someone could really hurt her if I don't do something."

"But what can you do? They're mortals, we're ghosts, Sam. What can you do?" Renata hugged herself.

I had never felt so helpless in my death. "I don't know," I said. "I dont know."

CHAPTER 16

I CAN RESIST ANYTHING BUT TEMPTATION

"AT THIS POINT," SAM SAID WHEN HE MATERIALIZED IN the passenger seat, "a smart person would head for the library and do a little research on that fire. It could have been arson. Busbee could collect the insurance and still screw his partners."

"As you have figured out by now," I replied, "I am not a smart person."

By that point I was operating on pure emotional adrenaline, which means that I had turned off my common sense.

"That was quite an interesting chat. What did Chinaberry mean about Busbee killing Renata?" Sam asked.

"I was wondering if you were lurking in the shrubbery. Who do you think you are, James Ghost Bond? I don't know if he was just mad at Busbee or if Busbee really did kill Renata. What do you think?"

"Ghost, James Ghost, at your service. I would call my parental units and try to see if they recalled anything about insurance or arson, if I were you," Sam suggested. "The clot sickens!"

"Having to deal with them—plus a bereaved and no doubt disturbed Jennifer at full actress speed—cancels the thought."

"Still, Chinaberry did accuse the late, great Busbee of killing his ex-wife. If I read all the signals correctly Chinaberry was a little sweet on Miss Renata himself and not too fond of the Busster. If you dislike someone it's natural to suspect the worst of them, up to and including murder," Sam said thoughtfully. His translucent form leaned back into the passenger seat and he closed his eyes, deep in thought or sleep; one never knows, do one?

"This puts Chinaberry into the general population of suspects, but it's hard to imagine a man who seems so ill trussing up a great big man like Busbee and dumping him overboard," he finally offered.

"Would Busbee have killed his ex-, or soon-to-be ex-, wife if she was going to go public with his insurance-fraud scheme? Blowing the whistle on an ex's transgressions is as common as hen tracks; ask anyone who works for the IRS," I suggested.

A thought hit me so hard that I almost slammed on the brakes right there in the westbound lane of Route 50, your Ocean Deathway.

"Suppose Renata had the goods on Busbee?" My mind, what there was of it, raced ahead. "If Renata came back and found Busbee had torched his failing hotel to collect the insurance, there wasn't much Busbee could do about it. So he—"

"So he kills his ex-wife," Sam interrupted. "He could

174

have killed Renata and sent her car off the bridge. But then how did he get back to the island that night?"

"Suppose Renata's death was a tragic accident on an icy bridge with no rails?"

"Then why kill Busbee thirty years later?" Sam asked reasonably. "Now suppose, just suppose, that he follows her to the Calais Bridge, then he stops her. They get into a big fight. He strangles her; we know he's an abuser, that's why she left him. So she's dead and his secret's safe. He weights down the accelerator pedal with the brick, and off the bridge Renata goes, never to be seen again for thirty years. And when she is found, all that's left is the major bones. Without soft tissue there's no way to tell how she died."

"Good script," I admitted. "Here's another one. Someone else—who is also ass-deep in the insurance scam—follows in a second car and gives Busbee a lift home. Someone like the Old Man or Billy Chinaberry. No tire tracks in the snow and ice, remember. That's how come no one knew Renata went off the bridge in the first place."

Sam whistled between his teeth. "Good. But why kill Busbee thirty years later?"

Had something been in that car all those years at the bottom of the river, something that had signed Clinton's death warrant?

Whoa! Watch it!" Sam cried.

A Chinaberry Royal Farms eighteen-wheeler passed me with a shriek of the air horn and I snapped back into drive mode.

There was something I needed to figure out, but it had eluded me. I cursed under my breath.

Sam sighed. "Tell ya what you need to do," he said. "Whyn't you go back and take another look at the

Cadillac? I've got a hunch."

"You and your hunches," I grumbled. "The last time you had a hunch I almost ended up burned alive."

"Trust me," Sam replied sunnily. "What can go wrong?"

Ha.

> *Gone to My Millisha Meeting*
> *Back at 4*
> *Larry*

Sam slowly spelled out the hand-lettered sign, just in case I'd missed any of the subtle nuances of Cousin Larry's literary musings.

LaMonte Auto Salvage and Recycling was closed up tighter than Larry's mind, but Walter trotted out to greet us with a snarl. Living or dead, he was not going to let anyone on his turf—except possibly my leg, upon which he still wanted to express his unrequited affection.

Fortunately, he was easily appeased with the crusts of an ancient Arch Deluxe and some cold, stiff fries from the vast store of trash that rides around in the back of my car.

"Walter is smarter than Larry, but that's not saying much," Sam muttered. I noted that not even a ghost wanted to pet a pit bull.

"At least when Walter humps your leg you know he's glad to see you, which is more than I can say for a lot of human males," I replied tartly.

"Nice doggy," Sam said, sliding easily through the wire gate." See, I can slip in like warm butter. Good doggie." Walter just gave him a disgusted look, as if the dead were beneath his notice. No legs to hump there, I guess.

As I clambered—preppy drag and all—over the chain-link fence, the dog greeted my leg in his usual enthusiastic fashion.

"Dammit, Walter! Down!" I snapped. He just looked at me with those big puppy-dog eyes until I dug an Altoid out of my pocketbook for him. Taking it, he evidently considered himself bribed, disengaging from me in order to chew on the mint. "You need a life even more than I do," I told him.

"There's the infamous Coupe de Ville of Death!" Sam exclaimed, running down the narrow alleyway between the stacks of junked cars.

Since I wasn't as twiglike or as buff as Jen, I had a little more trouble crawling through the shattered passenger window, but Walter kept me company by parking himself between the car and the gate, growling protectively. Sam just slid through the door, perching on the front seat. "Wow," he said, his voice muffled.

A few days of warm weather and sunlight had beaten back some of the fungus, but the faded, rotted-to-nothingness leather interior of the passenger compartment still smelled like a hundred thousand dead crabs rotting away on an August day. Springs from the seats poked at my legs as I crawled past the steering wheel, feeling around on the moist floor.

"Boy, they really knew how to build 'em back then, didn't they?" Sam asked cheerfully, pushing on the dead horn and pretending to steer the bent wheel. "I feel just like Elvis at Graceland."

"Yeah, you're both dead and you both have really bad taste."

I held my breath and groped a bit around the moldy backseat, but I didn't find anything. "I'm not even sure what I'm looking for. After thirty years underwater what would have been left? Besides, I'm pretty sure Jen and the techs have gone over everything with a fine-tooth comb," I muttered.

"Beep, beep, comin' through," Sam said happily. "Thank yew, thank yew verra much. Why," he asked me, turning around, "don't you check out the ashtrays in the backseat?"

Trust Sam. I'd forgotten that the old lead sleds had two small ashtrays in the back, one sunk into each armrest. The left one was missing, but the one on the right was still there, a small steel-lidded box with a tiny tab pull. It was corroded shut from years beneath the water, but I never climb into murdermobiles anywhere without my handy little Buck knife.

I pried the lid open with some effort and more damage to the rotten leather on the armrest. "If there's a waterlogged, thousand-year-old cigarette butt in here, I'm smoking it," I promised.

"Those things will kill you," Sam said. This from a ghost.

But instead of a cigarette, I saw a piece of metal.

I pried it out, examining it in the fight. "Damn, Sam! It's a key! Renata must have hidden it there!"

It was not more than a couple of inches long, one of those ornately headed shank keys people used to use to lock drawers in old cabinets. It was corroded and covered with verdigris, and I wiped it off on my skirt. The head glinted faintly in the light as I turned it this way and that.

"Does it took familiar?" Sam asked me.

At that moment Walter set up a furious barking, growling deep in his throat as he raced toward the junkyard gates.

I peered out of the shattered window in time to see a

shiny black car turn around and haul away down Red Toad Road in a hail of mud and gravel.

"Probably another dissatisfied customer," Sam suggested cheerfully.

"Let's get out of here before Larry comes back," I said, climbing out of the Coupe de Ville. "I don't want to get gunned down by some pack of armed and dangerous morons."

"Easy for you to say," Sam whistled cheerfully as he passed through the fence and stood waiting for me on the other side.

After disengaging Walter from my leg again, I hefted myself out of LaMonte Auto Salvage and Recycling the same way I had come in. It wasn't any easier the second time.

Back in my car, I studied the key. "This really looks familiar," I said at last. "I remember it from somewhere. I just can't remember where."

Sam grinned. "I've already helped you more than I should have. Maybe Jennifer remembers it," he suggested. "The key to the Ornamental Hermit. Quick, Hollis, the game is afoot!"

And with that he disappeared, just like he always does when things get interesting.

I found my father where I knew he would be, and I was not surprised that Jen was with him. Hanging around my father is much better than having my mother force you to wash and sort clothes for her rummage sales.

When he's upset Dad goes down to the harbor and putters around on his boat. He can futz with the engine or with his gear for hours; I think it soothes him, doing things like that. The house may be my mother's province, but his boat, that belongs to him alone.

He was baiting up when I approached him, cutting chunks of salt eel and tying them to the snoods of his trotlines, which he carefully wound into a plastic barrel. Jen was sitting on the stern washboard, incongruous in her expensive slacks and designer sweater. She smiled weakly when she saw me coming.

"I knew you'd show up, Hollis!" she said gratefully. She didn't look like a grieving daughter, but then again, her nonrelationship with Busbee hadn't been much to mourn for.

Dad looked up from beneath his Patamoke Seafood cap when he heard my voice, then looked down again. With a thin, sharp knife he chopped eel, the sound of the blade hitting the block loud in the afternoon stillness.

I hadn't realized how weather-beaten he looked, how the years of sun and water had turned his skin into crinkled leather, until I saw him that afternoon. He's getting old, I thought.

Silently and without invitation I boarded the workboat. The washboards dipped beneath my weight as I stepped down into the deck and perched uneasily on the engine house.

I decided it was better not to say anything and to let him take the lead. When he's in one of his moods he can just as easily tell me to get lost as let me in on what's going on in his mind. But I took the fact that Jennifer was there as a good sign.

The big old knife thunked heavily on the wooden board. A long, slithery eel coated with rock salt was neatly divided into four-inch chunks. The stench of rotting fish hung in a cloud around the boat.

I sat silently, watching my father's work-worn, callused hands, and thought about his life of heavy labor. They say being a waterman takes a strong mind and a weak back, but at that moment I realized how smart my father was.

"Mr. Perk, I think you need to tell Hollis what happened," Jen said gently in a low voice. "She's got a right to know."

"Dad, whatever it is you know that I—"

He suddenly looked up, and his old eyes—that clear blue, like a winter river—met mine. "I didn't kill him," he said abruptly.

Whack! Another chunk of eel fell away. My father drove the blade of the knife into the board.

"I didn't think you did," I said, indignant. "I'm trying to prove you didn't!"

He looked up. "I did toss the sumbitch overboard though." His gravelly voice rumbled deep in his chest. He picked up another eel, and it sprawled dead in his hand. He flopped it on the board. "Tied 'im all up and threw him overboard," he said matter-of-factly. "I went out there after work, in the boat, to reason with him. It's not right for a man to turn his back on his children! When I got out there I found him dead in the bathtub, floating facedown. Man taking a bath don't float facedown." He pulled up the knife and whacked at the eel. It split apart beneath the blade. "Good thing I took the boat too. No tire tracks. I seen that on *Hart to Hart*."

"Your dad did it to protect me, Hollis," Jen injected quickly. "He thought it would look as if I did it, and he didn't want me to be arrested for it."

"I thought, well, if they find him out in the water they'll figure he was thrown overboard. So I wrapped him all up in some wire I found in the kitchen, hauled him down to the boat, and took him away out there to the Swann's Island light and tossed him overboard. Threw the rest of the wire over too. Movin'

181

deadweight's tough; if I hadn't trussed him up I would't o' been able to pull 'im aboard. One way or the other he'd be drowned, that's all they'd know. A drowned man's lungs fill up with his own fluids. They can't tell if he drowned in fresh- or saltwater. I seen that on *Columbo.*" *My* father sounded proud of himself.

"You drowned Busbee in the bathtub?" I asked Jen.

She shook her head. "I'd walked out there to try and reason with him. . . . But he was dead when I got there. I panicked and ran back to tell your parents." She twisted her fingers together in her lap.

"And Friendly questioned all of you?"

"Don't worry, Mr. Perk's given your friend Friendly an alibi, as have we all. We were all together Thursday night, watching TV at your folks' house. I'll swear to that in court."

"Ain't nobody on this island will say any different, at least not to any foreigner," my father muttered. *Whack!* The knife came down again.

"When did you go out to Turkey Buzzard Point?" I asked Jennifer. Thursday night?"

"Thursday afternoon. He was already dead. He was stiff." Jennifer shuddered. "I touched him. He was cold and white and stiff. It was ugly. He was already starting to . . . attract flies."

Whack!

My father looked up at me. "I waited till Friday evening, then dumped him overboard. As far as the police know I was out checking my lay. There's been some thefts around here, people stealing trotlines right out o' the river." He looked up. "How the hell was I to know you were out there too? The last thing I wanted was for my own daughter to be there when they pulled him out of the water." My father sounded fierce. I knew

182

he was sorry. Sorry wasn't enough.

"Dad, that's hindering!" I almost yelped.

"So?" My father asked. He really didn't get it.

"You can get in a lot of trouble tampering with a corpse and a homicide investigation. What got into you?" I demanded, exasperated.

"I woulda done the same if it were you or Robbie," he said gruffly. "Mainland law ain't the same as island law."

I had no reply for that.

"It could have been an accident, or a heart attack or something," I sighed. "Maybe it was natural and you just panicked or something."

"Not with all those bruises on him," my father growled. *Whack!* Another chunk of eel rolled across the board. "Don't you say a word to your mother; I won't have it," Dad pronounced. *Whack!*

"She'll find out soon enough when the cops drag you off to jail," I snapped. "Jesus, Dad. I mean, what the hell were you two thinking?"

"They won't think anything if you don't say anything," Jen said cheerfully.

I opened and closed my mouth and nothing came out. I was stumped and stunned. I sputtered a bit, I'll admit. They really had no idea how much trouble they were in. Trying to explain it to them was as useless as trying to justify the existence of Prince Charles.

But I felt honor bound to at least try. "What have you two done? Don't you know how much trouble you can get into?"

"We won't if you don't say anything," Jen repeated reasonably. "We have our alibi."

"That's right," my father agreed. "We Beddoe's Islanders stick together!"

183

It did cross my mind that the two of them could have killed him; I have long ago stopped being surprised at anything done by anyone at any time. If they had killed Busbee it would behoove me to just pack it all in, toss the key overboard, and forget the whole thing. As you may have figured out by now, I am morally elastic. It's my Beddoe's Island blood.

But I was damned if I'd see my father in jail. I took a deep breath and counted to ten.

"So," I said at last in a careful, casual voice. "We'll assume you didn't kill Busbee. Who did? If, indeed, he was killed and didn't have a heart attack from eating peanut butter out of the jar?"

"We were hoping Friendly would have told you," Jen said, smiling at me uncertainly. I really don't think they had any idea of how much trouble they could be in, and I hated being the one to tell them.

"I don't have a clue. Dad, you said he was all bruised when you saw him. What kind of bruises?"

"All round his legs and ankles. Big, ugly bruises. It was coming on to dark, and I was more interested in getting him trussed up and into the boat than taking a good look at 'im. He was ugly alive and he was uglier dead. A dead body is deadweight; you have to really *heft* that sucker. Had to haul 'im all the way down the boat too. Couldn't drag 'im, that would have left marks, on the ground. I seen that on *Matlock* once."

He sounded so proud of himself.

Jen could have killed Busbee, but I couldn't see how she could have drowned him in the bathtub. He was a big strong man, and she would have been covered with bruises and scratches because he would have struggled. One look at her face and her bare arms and you could see she wasn't injured. Nor for that matter was my dad.

I felt a vast sense of relief. It's not a pleasant thought, the idea that your oldest friend or your father could kill someone.

"Have an Altoid," Jen said, producing the red and white box. Her false eyelashes fluttered daintily.

I pulled out the key, showing it to her in the palm of my hand.

"What does this go to?" I asked. "Do you know?"

She picked it up between two long fingernails, squinting at it in the sunlight.

"What's this?" she asked. "It looks like the key to the old curio cabinet in the parlor, doesn't it?"

Bingo. Double bingo, triple bingo! Bells and whistles!

"Come with me," I said. "I think I know what the Ornamental Hermit is. I just don't know why!"

"You comin' home for dinner?" my father asked. "Mom's making crab cakes tonight."

"I haven't thought about that thing in years! I was looking for gold and jewels!"

"This is probably worth a lot more, at least to someone," I told her grimly. "Someone who doesn't want to be known."

When we arrived at Turkey Buzzard Point the Clinton homeplace was sealed off with police tape. Busbee's purple Eldorado sat beside the house, shiny and sleek. But the property was not the focal point of morbid curiosity seekers. Since no one knew Busbee had been murdered here, there would seem to be no reason for undue attention, but you never know. It was safe to assume that their main enemy having been eliminated, the crabbers were back out on the water again—rather than helping themselves, as some of them were wont to

185

do, to the stuff Busbee had lying around that he wouldn't be using anymore.

Unless, of course, they have crabbing in hell, which I seriously doubt, no matter how cussed crab behavior can be.

"The police were here Saturday morning. I gave them permission to look the place over," Jen told me. "They took away all of Father's ledgers, letters, and tax returns and stuff I think they were looking for a financial clue."

As I parked my car out of sight behind the cinderblock building that had once been the packing house, I felt that something was somehow wrong. It was quiet—too quiet. Not even a bird sang, and the lonesome rumble of a loose tin roof somewhere was muffled, like distant thunder.

"I have a key to the kitchen door." Jen and I skirted around the police tape wrapping the crumbling Victorian and walked up the rotting back steps.

The door squealed back on the hinges as we entered the empty kitchen. Nothing seemed to have changed since I had been there with Jennifer last Monday. It seemed like a lifetime ago that I had watched the Old Man and Billy Chinaberry confront Busbee right in this room.

Jen shivered. "This is giving me the creeps. It reminds me of the time that Carla inherited that creepy old mansion in Payne Valley that turned out to be haunted . . . ."

"Uh-huh." There were still dirty dishes in the sink, and the open jar of store-brand peanut butter was on the table. An early fly was feasting on a piece of toast.

Busbee's clothing was piled on a chair beside the bathroom door, and his ratty terry-cloth robe lay on the floor, half in and half out of the bathroom. I peered in and frowned, noting that the tub was filled with gray water, as if Busbee had been interrupted while taking one of his many baths.

The wallpaper behind the tub was stained with watermarks. I went in, looking at the old clawfoot tub. It was full of gray water.

"The curio cabinet!" Jen exclaimed. She held up the key.

"We have to work fast," I said, turning away. "There's no telling when the cops'll be back, and I sure as hell don't want to be caught here when Friendly and company return!"

We walked quickly into the parlor. "I'll bet we're the first people in this room in ages. Someone who has no friends has no need for a parlor in which to entertain them," Jen murmured.

I looked around at the big old carved mahogany and walnut pieces. The rigid sofa, the formal chairs, the desk, the armoire, the Welsh dresser were all still shrouded in dusty sheets. If you're the most-hated man in your neighborhood, I guess you *don't* need a place to entertain visitors, and God knows, Busbee was too cheap to hire a cleaning lady.

Jen headed directly for the curio cabinet filled with Busbee's grandmother's Bristol glass vases and Chelsea bow figurines. They were probably untouched since the days that Jen and I would carefully take them down and play all a rainy afternoon with ceramic milkmaids and small painted dogs.

Neither Miss Renata nor Busbee had much use for "that old stuff," as they called it. Their tastes ran toward the garishly modern. And besides, half the time they were fighting rather than paying any attention to two little girls. I suddenly recalled their low, angry voices with a shiver.

In my mind's eye I saw a tiny Jen climbing up on the swan-neck rocker to take a key down from its place on the mantel so that we could unlock the glass-front doors of the curio cabinet to get to the figurines.

Now she was sliding the old key into the lock on the cabinet once again; it turned the tumblers and the doors swung open. No one had dusted these for years; the faint smell of dry rot spilled out at me, and I coughed on the layers of spiderwebs and grimy motes that floated out at us.

Neither of us spoke; we were too excited. The search for the Ornamental Hermit was almost at an end. Piece by piece we carefully removed the seashells that said *Souvenir of Colonial Beach,* the crudely painted bric-a-brac, the blown-glass animals, the fussy little vases and knickknacks of two generations past, placing them on the cracked surface of a marble-topped table that had seen better days. It was as if Busbee's grandmother was watching us, waiting for us to break one of her bibelots.

No doubt they were worth a good deal of money now as antiques themselves, but not even the Roseville cachepots and candlesticks were what we were seeking.

My fingers touched something and I exclaimed.

It had been taped to the back wall of the cabinet, well-hidden behind a brittle china doll whose silk dress crumbled to dust at my touch. But the tape was old and dried out, and it came away in my hand without resistance. I pulled out the round ceramic object and we stared at it.

It was a painted Chelsea figurine, no more than a few inches tall. A tiny man with a beard and a tricorn hat, leaning on a staff. Around the base of the little statuette the words *Stephen Duck* had been painted in gilt. A large piece of the puzzle into place.

"So that's the Ornamental Hermit," Jen breathed.

"I wondered if maybe it wasn't something that came up with Renata's car that had killed Busbee," I said. "Maybe it was something that was not in the car that should have been there, something like this? Look, there's some paper wadded up inside it!"

"I'll take that," a voice said behind us.

CHAPTER 17

NASTY SURPRISES

JEN AND I SLOWLY TURNED AROUND.

"I warned you to stay away from this, Hollis. No good can come of dredging this up." H. P. Wescott smiled at me in a way I wasn't quite sure I liked. "I came out here to check on my . . . reputation. I want to be sure my name isn't involved in this. What are you two doing here?"

"I'm trying to right some old wrongs," I snapped. "And keep innocent people from getting themselves into this any deeper."

He was examining the small figurine with the same look of wonder I'd felt. "What is this?" he asked.

"It's the Ornamental Hermit. Stephen Duck. Ornamental hermits were a novelty in eighteenth-century gardens, when this figurine was made. Duck was evidently quite famous in his day . . . ." Thank you, Ed Poe, I thought; you're better than the Internet.

H.P. snorted. "A cheap china doodad!" He handed it back to me. "That's what all the fuss was about? Just a cheap china figure?"

I turned it over. It was hollow, but inside there was a slip of paper. Gingerly, I pulled it out. It was yellowed and crisp with age, but the handwriting was precise and clean. A bookkeeper's script.

"On February 12, 1968, 1 witnessed my estranged husband, Busbee L. Clinton, start the fire that destroyed the Bayside Hotel. He created an electric fire by exposing several wires in the kitchen fixtures. I believe that he committed arson in order to collect the insurance money on the hotel. If anything happens to me, call the police. I am writing this because I am afraid he will kill me—"

"Give me that!" H.P. snatched it out of my hand and read through it quickly. He seemed much calmer as he handed it to Jennifer.

"What's your interest in all of this?" I demanded. "How did you know that it existed?"

"Renata told me. I didn't know where it was," H.P. said, "or even if it really existed. There are all kinds of laws, and we could have ended up in big trouble, Chinaberry and me. Arson is a serious business, and so is insurance fraud. Clinton burned down the Bayside to collect the insurance, but Chinaberry and I didn't have anything to do with that, and you can't prove we did." He smiled sourly. "Our names aren't on there."

"What else didn't you tell me about?" I demanded.

"Why don't you two sit down," H.P. growled.

What the Old Man wants, the Old Man gets. I sat on one of the sheet-covered chairs. Clouds of dust rose up around me. Gingerly, Jen sat down opposite me. "I can't believe this!" she exclaimed.

"That's it," H.P. said. "After all these years, damn Busbee's hide!" He grumbled, then sat down heavily in a carved armchair, regarding us resentfully.

"I think you owe Jen some explanation. She's been through thirty years of hell, you know," I told him.

The Old Man nodded to Jen. "I guess there's no harm in telling you now," he said. "When your mother came down here for the last time, she called Chinaberry and she called me. She wanted money to start a new life, as far from Busbee as she could get. She was willing to trade for her evidence that Busbee burned down the hotel to collect the insurance. Can you imagine what an arson charge could have done to Billy and me as businessmen in this community? Even if we weren't directly involved, something like that could have really damaged our reputations. No one would want to do business with us." He grimaced. "Even you can understand that, Hollis."

"Blackmail?"

"That's a hard word to use where Renata was concerned," H.P. sighed. "She was the kind of woman who made you want to do things for her." He almost smiled like a real human being. "She said if anything happened to her to look for the Ornamental Hermit. But she didn't tell us what it was."

"A china figurine," Jen said.

"When your mother disappeared," he told her, "everyone assumed that it was an accident. When the car was recovered and there wasn't even any trace of anything vaguely resembling an Ornamental Hermit, Chinaberry. and I thought Busbee had screwed us over. Again. I'm sorry about your father, but . . . he was a no-good blackmailing bastard who deserved to die, frankly." That was the Old Man, a master of tact and sympathy.

"Was she murdered, Mr. Wescott?"

The Old Man shrugged. "Chinaberry always thought

191

so. He was certain that your father killed Renata. Busbee never liked to give anything up. Then, when she turned up in that car thirty years later . . .well, you figure it out."

"Please don't tell me you killed Busbee," I told H.P. "I don't want to know if you did."

A smile played over his face as he contemplated the idea.

"I wish I had killed the son of a bitch, but no, I didn't do it." He snapped back into H.P. mode again. "I do hope, Ms. Clinton, that you and I can come to some sort of a deal about acquiring Buzzard Point. Your father and I had come to an arrangement, and as his heir I hope you and I can continue—"

"Excuse me," someone said.

The three of us jumped as if we'd been bitten, but Jen let out a scream. "That's him! That's the stalker!" she shrieked.

CHAPTER 18

FISH OR CUT BAIT

THERE'S ONE THING I HAVE ALWAYS FOUND interesting about America: Everyone is armed and dangerous. I was going into my bag for my .38 (never track a murder without it), and H.P. produced a .357 Bodyguard. If Jen had a LadySmith we could have started a shootout at the Clinton Corral.

The newcomer quickly raised his arms in the air.

"Stalker?" he squeaked.

Well, he didn't look much like what I thought a stalker should took like. He was tall, thin, and blond,

192

with a trendy ponytail, an earring, and a very modish black leather jacket. He looked more like a *Vanity Fair* model, with a dimple in his chin so deep you could have hidden a Life Savers in it.

"Stalker! Eighty-six, Jen! That is so beat," he said in hurt tones, starting to put his hands on his hips in a gesture of disgust.

"Keep 'em high in the sky, bunk." The Old Man waved his gun, and the blonde quickly raised his hands.

"Well, I mean, really!" the new man muttered.

Jen sat down again. "You're right, Peter," she sighed. "He's not a stalker."

The Old Man squinted at him. "Hell, no, that's Stud Ridge! I thought you were in jail!"

"Stud Ridge is the character I play on *Hapless Hearts*. He's in jail, for the moment," the blonde said through chattering teeth. "My name is Peter Porter. I'm Jen's SO."

"S.O.?" the Old Man asked suspiciously.

"Significant Other," Peter Porter explained. "Her boyfriend."

I was still a few sentences back, trying to absorb the idea that the Old Man was a faithful *Hapless Hearts* watcher.

"It's true. Peter's my boyfriend, not a stalker. There is no stalker. I made the whole thing up," Jen sighed. "Although Peter has been doing a bit of spying on everyone behind the scenes."

The Old Man seemed more disappointed that he couldn't shoot someone than surprised at this interesting twist.

"Can I put my hands down now?" Peter asked.

H.P. reluctantly holstered his weapon. "Son, I think you and Jennifer owe us an explanation," he said.

"Are you all right?" the actor asked Jen as he sat down on the dusty sofa beside her. Great. Just what I needed. Two actors in one room and one old man watching *Hapless Hearts*. And a partridge in a pear tree.

"You see, I wasn't certain who I could trust," Jen explained.

"So we decided that I would play behind the scenes. Sort of dig the dirt, you know. I once played a private detective. Maybe you saw *Skrawkoski, P.I.* in the ninety-five season? It was only on for five episodes before the network yanked it, but—"

"Do you drive a black car?" I asked.

"Am I that bad at tailing people?" he asked, genuinely hurt. "Yeah, I rented a black car. I've been staying at a motel on Route 50, the Lock and Load? And sort of looking out for Jennifer behind the scenes, like a stage manager."

"You!" the Old Man suddenly exclaimed. "I recognize your voice. You were the one who called me and said you were Busbee Clinton and I'd better get on out here! I'll be damned!"

"And Peter was the one who called Mr. Perk and Father on Sunday too," Jennifer said.

Peter Porter looked rather hurt. "I thought I did a pretty good job with his voice," he said.

"We needed to get Father out of the house so Peter could have a look around," Jennifer explained. "While he was at your house Sunday fighting with Mr. Perk, Peter was doing a quick look around at the books and financial records."

"Waste of time. I couldn't find anything that related to Jennifer's mother. And the dust in this place is bad for my allergies."

"Oh, my poor honey bunny," Jennifer cooed, and the

194

two of them sort of mooned at each other, holding hands and nuzzling until I thought I was going to be ill.

"I'd do anything for my honey bunny," Peter crooned into her hair. "I'd run lines with my baby anytime."

The Old Man looked as if he wanted to shoot both of them. It was an accident. The only thing worse than an actor's love affair with self is an actor in love with another actor.

"So!" H.P. said loudly. "Back to the subject at hand. You called me and you called Chinaberry and got us out here. Why?"

"So I could see how you all reacted together, of course," Jen said, tearing herself away from Peter's lips. "To see if anyone acted guilty."

"Oh, for heaven's sake," I muttered.

"Did *you* kill Busbee, by any chance?" H.P. asked Peter hopefully.

The actor shook his head. "No, of course not. I've never played a murderer! Thursday night I was on the phone with my agent practically all night. She's negotiating a TV movie of the week for Jennifer and me, based on Jennifer's life story. That should be easy to check."

"I'll sue," the Old Man and I both said at once.

I turned the ceramic figure over in my hands and looked at the note again. Almost all of the pieces of the puzzle had fallen into place. All save one.

I jumped to my feet. "If you didn't kill Busbee I think I know who did," I said. "I'm out of here!"

"I'm coming with you!" Jen said, rising. "This is my mother we're talking about!"

"Now, Hollis," the Old Man rumbled, "don't go off half-cocked!"

But I was out of there before they could pursue me.

195

CHAPTER 19

EXTREME UNCTUOUSNESS

WATER GARDEN WAS IN THE GATHERING SHADOWS OF evening when I drove up. A breeze from the river ruffled through thousands of tulips planted around the gardens, but the Lincoln was gone. As I walked up to the front door the wind sent a chill through my thin sweater.

Nonetheless, I knocked smartly on the chicken knocker and, when there was no answer, ducked around the house through the ornate shrubbery and past the rooster fountain.

The greenhouse door was unlocked. I cautiously let myself in, and once again the heavy smell of growing green things and rotting vegetation assailed my senses.

There were dim grow lights illuminating the conservatory, but not very well. Shadows stood in wait. The fronds of the aralia palms looked like grasping fingers.

"Mr. Chinaberry?" I called.

Only the distant sound of dripping water answered me.

The blooming potted tulips stretched out around me in orderly rows.

They reminded me of the pod people in *Invasion of the Body Snatchers*. I half expected space aliens to start hatching out of them as I walked past, pod humans who would reach out and drag me down to my vegetable transformation.

A good imagination is a curse.

I made my way through the dim room, and when

something wet and slick brushed my face I almost screamed.

It was the frond of a staghorn fern in a hanging basket.

Mentally cursing, I groped my way forward.

"I thought you might come back."

I spun around.

Billy Chinaberry, the Poultry Prince, moved in the shadows.

He looked very sick as he stepped into the light. He had to lean on a bench to support himself. "Did you bring Jennifer or the police?" he asked me.

"Neither. I came alone."

"Ah. Well then." He wiped his hands on his apron. He must have been working with his tulips. Beneath the dim light he was gray, and the bags under his eyes were purplish. But his debility could have been an act. I needed to be cautious.

"We found the Ornamental Hermit. It was a little china figurine, and Renata had stuffed a confession into it about Busbee setting the fire that burned down the Bayside."

He nodded, but I could tell by his thousand-mile stare that he wasn't especially concerned about that. "Humor an old man," he said. "Let's walk out to the maze."

He gave me his arm and I took it, but it was he who leaned on me for support.

In the blue spring twilight the gardens looked peaceful and precise. We made our way slowly along the garden pathways. Over our heads the pink blossoms dipped and waved. The white marble statues gazed with blind eyes. The water in the fountain splashed and bubbled.

"Do you appreciate irony, Ms. Ball?" Chinaberry

asked me.

"No one does it better," I replied softly.

"Then you will understand what a terrible irony it is to be dying when all the world is just coming alive again—"

"Yes," I said. A gray melancholy, never far from the surface, suffused my mood.

We turned into the maze. The high boxwood walls cut off the wind; it was almost warmer in there. It felt safe and private in a world where you don't get too much of either one.

"My suspicions were confirmed, then."

"What suspicions?"

"That Busbee killed Renata."

"How did you figure that?"

"Busbee was a miser. He never let go of anything. All that Clinton cared about was money. This is what I believe happened. Renata knew what he had done, so he followed her car in a rage to Calais Bridge. Either he managed to run her off the bridge, or he stopped her there and killed her somehow. He would have killed her rather than allow her to leave, especially if she had evidence that would have put him behind bars. He weighted down the accelerator with the brick and sent Renata, car and all, over the bridge."

"It could have happened that way," I agreed. "He could have gotten away with murder—if the car hadn't been found, if Jen hadn't found that brick." We turned left, then right, then left again.

We came to the heart of the maze and sat down on the bench. I told him everything I knew and everything I suspected. Well, almost everything. I left my father out of it.

When I had finished he merely nodded.

198

For a long time neither of us said anything. Chinaberry was remembering, and I was drained.

Then he finally spoke. "I have had a lot of time to think lately. I don't sleep all that well, you see. The pain keeps me awake long into the night." He coughed. "Until they found Renata I believed she had simply taken off. Perhaps she had panicked. But when they found her and there was nothing that could have been the Ornamental Hermit in the car, I knew in my heart Clinton had killed her.

"Either one of us—Wescott or I—is Jennifer's father. We were both crazy about Renata. She had that effect on men, you know; she was something of a *femme fatale*. We were both, unknown to the other, carrying on with her! So when she said she was pregnant and one of us was the father, we were at a bit of a standstill. You see, this was the sixties, and we were both married; something like this could have ruined our reputations. She wouldn't hear of an abortion." He sighed. "We finally decided, you see, that she could marry Busbee. But his price was the Bayside Hotel. So of course we became investors. It was a form of blackmail, but it worked."

"That's why she called both of you to ask for money."

"She had that right. And we would have given it to her without question. Who do you think paid for Jennifer's upkeep and schooling all those years? Every six months we paid Busbee, and he forwarded the money on to Rochester. It was the least we could do, but good Lord, to be trapped in a hellacious bargain with that man—"

I put my hand on his. His flesh was cold. "If you hadn't killed him, Mr. Chinaberry, someone else would have," I said gently.

He gave me a thin smile and patted the hand that lay on top of his. "You have a reprehensible sense of humor, Ms. Ball," he chuckled.

"So you killed Busbee to avenge Renata," I said aloud, and startled myself, because I had only meant to think it.

"It's amazing what you can do when you're angry enough," Chinaberry observed matter-of-factly. "When I drove over there Thursday morning to have it out with him, I wasn't certain what I meant to do. But I found him in the bathtub." He sighed and it turned into a strangled cough. "Many years ago I read about a British murderer who did away with a series of wives by drowning them in the bathtub. 'The Brides-in-the-Bath Murderer,' he was called. It was a very simple method. He grasped the women by the ankles and pulled them under the water. They were helpless, and they drowned. It took a great deal of cunning and a near-disastrous experiment for Scotland Yard to solve the case, as I recall. Isn't it interesting what tricks your memory can play on you? Some days I can't recall what I ate for lunch, but a newspaper story from fifty years ago, that I remembered."

He coughed, a great racking spasm. From a pocket he withdrew a handkerchief and spit blood into it, wadding it up in his hand.

The moon, a crescent of silver, was rising in the evening sky.

"It wasn't that hard to do, actually," he said when he recovered himself "It didn't take a great deal of strength. Clinton was physically in worse shape than I am. All I had to do was grab his ankles and pull hard and hang on while he struggled. But it did take

200

endurance. Endurance I had. The whole time I was holding him and watching his struggle for breath, all I saw was Renata struggling in that car, under the water."

"But Daz . . . the person who found him said he was floating facedown."

"Well, I had to turn him over to be sure that he was dead. He was. Oh, he was. I haven't been right since, but at least I'll die knowing that I did what I had to do, what I should have done thirty years ago."

I leaned back and closed my eyes. It was almost dark now. From somewhere I could hear the mournful coo of a whippoorwill.

"I've thought of making a provision for Jennifer in my will. That's one thing that won't be in the obituary: Jennifer. She looks so much like her mother. . . .I used to tune in just to watch her on that story, it was like seeing Renata all over again."

"Jennifer will be okay; she's a successful actress. Busbee probably has the first nickel he ever made. And selling Turkey Buzzard Point will net her a pretty good sum."

I felt infinitely weary.

"I don't think she needs to know. Of course, if you call the police she'll have to know," Chinaberry suggested cannily.

I opened my eyes and looked at a dying old man who didn't deserve to spend his last days with cops and courts and lawyers and tabloid-TV-show reporters. Maybe it wasn't the kind of justice you could find in a court. But then again, I don't always see eye to eye with the courts and the law; I'm a Beddoe's Islander myself. As I've noted elsewhere, I can be morally ambiguous.

"You know," I said, "you were talking about how memory can play tricks on you. I can't remember the

201

conversation we just had. But it's getting awfully cold. Why don't you let me help you inside, where you can get yourself settled for the evening?"

"Sounds like a good idea," Chinaberry grinned. "Tonight's *Murder, She Wrote* night on cable, and I never miss that."

As we walked across the lawns toward the house, I thought I saw Sam in the long shadows. And I thought I saw another ghost—the revenant of a woman with big hair and dangling earrings—smiling at me, but I knew it was just a trick of the light.

A ragged cloud crossed the silver moon and they were gone.

"That's exactly what happened," Renata said to me. I had never seen her so at peace. I knew she didn't have much time left here. I knew she would be going on to the rest she deserved after those thirty years under the water.

"Sometimes things work out in strange ways, I told her.

The bracelets on her wrists jangled and her dark hair shimmered in the moonlight of the mortal world. "He forced my car off the road." Renata shivered. "When I found out what he'd done to my daughter, I took her and ran—I've been punished enough, perhaps, but why did she have to be punished, by losing her mother?"

"That's not for me to judge," I said. "In the end we all have to live with the consequences of our own actions. Anyway, it seems Jennifer is doing all right for herself. Let the living sort it all out."

"Thank you. Sam. And thank Hollis too. She may not know how much you still love her, but she needs you. . ."

202

Renata had begun to fade.
I held out my hand.
She reached for it, but she was already gone.

CHAPTER 20

THE END OF THE GAME

USUALLY, WHEN IT RAINS, READING THE SUNDAY papers with Friendly is fun for me. I like the comics and the long, lazy Sunday afternoons spent browsing the book reviews and the features. I like it that Friendly will read out loud to me.

Until the afternoon he read the obituary I'd been dreading.

" 'Mr. Chinaberry will be buried at Mount Olivet Cemetery on Tuesday. Services will be private—' Are you okay?"

My own words were coming back to haunt me this gray November day. I listened to them and suddenly became more aware of the rain hitting the windows and the crackle of the fire in the wood-burning stove.

Friendly looked down at me. I had my head in his lap and was munching on some of the popcorn he'd just made. Until he read Billy Chinaberry's obit I'd been enjoying myself enormously. It's not every day someone comes over to my house with a stack of old Robert Mitchum movies and reads me the comics and rubs my head too. A girl reporter could get used to this, I had been thinking until that moment.

"I'm okay," I replied.

There was a silence, and I knew what Friendly was thinking before he even said it.

203

"I still can't figure it out. We find the corpse in saltwater, but the M.E. says he drowned in freshwater. It's the damned edema and the damned osmotic balance. They run the same test three times and it still comes out the same: Clinton drowned in freshwater. . . . But it's that wire that bothers me. It was the same kind of wire that was wrapped around that brick Jennifer Clinton found in the car . . . ."

Did I feel guilty? More than a little. And sad too. Sad for Billy Chinaberry, whose chickens and black tulips didn't buy him happiness; and for Jen, who was deprived of a mother; and for Renata Clinton, who never saw her daughter grow up. And angry at Busbee Clinton, who'd committed a cold-blooded murder and lived with it for thirty years. Moral ambiguity isn't always a comfortable place for me to be. But sometimes the law, in all its black-and-white magnificence, doesn't dispense justice. The law is words, a code of conduct for a so-called civilized society. I'd seen enough rich guilty people buy justice and enough poor innocent people jailed to have grown cynical about the law.

Besides, I'm from Beddoe's Island, where the law is an ass.

Still, that was the moment I could have, should have told Friendly about Billy Chinaberry's confession. I knew that sooner or later my silence would come back to haunt me. But I was between a rock and a hard place. I didn't want my father involved in a fight that wasn't his; he could face criminal charges. And he wasn't rich enough to buy justice, the way Billy Chinaberry could have done. I decided to let it die with Chinaberry. For Friendly it was just a part of his job. For my father it was his whole life that could be split apart. I kept silent.

Everyone has secrets. There are a lot of things in his

past that Friendly gets right fuzzy about, and I try not to push it too hard. Everyone needs some space, and if they don't get it they feel uncomfortable. Still, I knew he wasn't going to give up easily. He's not the type.

I'd cope with that when and if the time came. I was starting to feel as if I could like and trust this man, and that hadn't happened to me in a long time.

"Kiss me," I said, since that is usually a good way to change the subject to something we're both interested in.

It worked this time too.

And that's what they were doing when I sort of dropped by Holl's house. Just dropping by, checking in, and that's what I found. She was kissing that cop!

I stood there for a few moments, thinking.

Then I decided that Hollis must be feeling rather bored.

There was nothing, I thought, that would take her out of it faster than a good adventure.

I went to see what trouble I could get her into next.

"You know?" Friendly said to me when we came up for air. "I don't believe in ghosts, but sometimes I could swear your house is haunted."

Dear Reader:

I hope you enjoyed reading this Large Print mystery. If you are interested in reading other Beeler Large Print Mystery titles or any other Beeler Large Print titles, ask your librarian or write to me at

Thomas T. Beeler, *Publisher*
Post Office Box 659
Hampton Falls, New Hampshire 03844

You can also call me at 1-800-251-8726 and I will send you my latest catalogue.

Audrey Lesko chooses the titles I publish in Large Print. Our aim is to provide good books by outstanding authors—books we both enjoyed reading and liked well enough to want to share. We warmly welcome any suggestions for new titles and authors.

Sincerely,